CAN I HAVE A HUG FIRST?

Story Collection

By

Mary Paula Hunter

Dedicated to Katherine and Peter

TABLE OF CONTENTS

CAN I HAVE A HUG FIRST?

CAN I HAVE A HUG FIRST?

A gust of wind knocked me into a man who also hesitated in front of Gold's Gym.

"Sorry," I said, giving him a quick once-over, praying I hadn't maimed him. He frowned, glancing at a rush of clouds and the tops of trees thrashing back and forth. Minutes before, we had climbed one step after the next on side-by-side stair masters. I hope he hadn't seen me flinch when his sweat flew my way.

"Good luck," he said before bolting to the parking lot. I wanted to yell "thank you" for not being injured by my clumsiness and for having the kind of brain, like my husband's, that sticks to one thing at a time and doesn't connect the rarely connectable. Instead, I hurried off as an inverted black umbrella flew by. My first ballet class was in an hour, and I had to get home to change into my teaching clothes.

I walked at a fast clip, pushed by the wind while being pelted by flying debris and dirt along the main drag called Hope Street. The Hope Club, Hope Street, Hope Village--*Providence is obsessed with hope*, I thought, and then, about a block in front of me, a branch crashed to the sidewalk. I checked out the other trees lining the street as I waited for the light to change at the intersection of Hope and Benevolent. I was about a half mile from the single-family house we'd bought recently, holding onto our first house, a double-decker my husband and I hoped would provide the steady income we desperately needed.

"What do absentee landlords do?" my husband had asked, while frowning, the morning we drove to the closing. I knew he had a point. Neither of us had the faintest understanding of how to manage a property. Two units suddenly seemed like way more than one. But how complicated could it be?

"I think we just continue to fix things," I said, which seemed like a small price to pay for the relief of coming home to an empty house. The possibility of running into the inscrutable upstairs tenant had filled me with dread. All my skills of instantly morphing into a fake doppelganger deserted me whenever we met in the hall, her eyes narrowing at every word I uttered.

"Just keep going," I said to my husband as he coaxed our dying car into gear. "We don't want to be late," I said, praying there'd be no glitch in refinancing one property for the purchase of another.

On moving day, we rented the bottom apartment to two women who appeared out of nowhere while we lugged our Salvation Army furniture to a van we'd borrowed. As we drove away, my husband worried about renting to complete strangers.

"They seem reliable," I said, trying to remember their names. Midge and something else.

Before I turned left on Friendship, I heard my name, or a version of it. Devi, the Cambodian woman who cuts hair in the neighborhood, ran across the street waving at me. I worried she needed help translating something. She often mimed her half of our conversations. During one hair appointment, I'd given directions to someone on speakerphone as she held my head under a too hot stream of water. I thought about changing hair cutters, but I liked that she rushed through the wash, cut, and blow dry. Sometimes I left with damp hair.

"Everything bad," she said. I nodded, widening my eyes. I love hearing stories about someone's bad luck. "My son in ICU at hospital."

"Why?" I asked.

"He weigh four hundred and fifty pounds," she said, scrolling on her phone to a picture of an obese man strapped to a bed with wires coming from his face, neck, everywhere.

"I have a friend who works at Weight Watchers," I offered.

"If he live, you bring me friend."

"Oh Devi, I'll pray for him," I lied, or I sort of lied because as I ran off, waving to her, I actually tried out praying. But I couldn't pronounce his name or remember his particular affliction. And how do you pray for someone so fat? I guess I could pray that he ramps up his will power.

"Please, God," I said but was interrupted by a guy honking at a woman jaywalking. She backed up when another car came careening around the corner, screeching and swerving, missing her by an inch. *I'll never jaywalk again*, I thought, imagining this woman splayed on the cement, bleeding from everywhere like the wires attached to Devi's son. She stumbled around the corner and then hung on to a tree like she might pass out. I paused while wind whipped around me. As a witness, should I run to her? Make sure she's not suffering a stroke or an aneurysm? I pictured a headline demanding the whereabouts of a witness who'd left the scene of a potential homicide.

Then, just as I let Devi's son, this about-to-be-dead woman, and my possible incarceration go by the wayside, a clown ran toward me on my street—a very thin clown with a bright orange afro.

"I was knocking on your door," the clown yelled, waving both hands at me. I squinted hard. *Why two hands*, I thought. Was this a joke or a dream? Panic struck, and I worried the moment had arrived when I'd turn into something else. I wished I'd never heard the story of Daphne trapped inside a tree for eternity or the pizza delivery man trapped in an elevator in the South Bronx for a weekend. Maybe I was hallucinating? Had someone drugged me? The guy at the gym seemed benign, but my husband's cousin came to on a boulevard in Los Angeles minus his shoes and wallet after what he said was a friendly encounter. Probably involving women and alcohol, but still.

Luckily, the clown turned into my tenant--one of the two women in the bottom unit. I sighed, relieved to discover that I was still me with my mind intact.

"I need to talk to you," she yelled, even though she was about an inch from my face.

"What is wrong?" I asked.

"I don't feel safe in the apartment. Midge is abusive and also scary." She whispered the part about Midge being scary. I had seen this Midge at CVS and she didn't seem the least scary. Also, the clown-look made me wonder about this woman's sanity. Had we rented our apartment to an insane person? Why did she find me a kindred soul, and how did she know where we lived? I always picked up the rent from a milk box on their front porch.

"I must teach," I said, backing up, hoping I didn't seem uncaring. I didn't want criminal charges brought against me for callousness or indifference. For a second, I pictured myself stuck in a jail cell while my husband begged his brother for bail money, and I started to feel dizzy.

"Could you come to our house tonight so we can discuss this situation?" I asked. "My husband will be home, and if you're afraid of your roommate, we shouldn't come to you. I mean you shouldn't be in the apartment."

"Yes," she said. "I'll come. But can I have a hug first?"

"Of course," I said, inching away as she reached her arms toward me, letting her bag clunk to the sidewalk.

"Oh, your bag," I said, skirting around her, hugging her in a fake way so that we barely touched. "Good luck," I said. "And we'll see you tonight at eight?"

"Eight is good," she said. "But in the meantime, I will go to the library where I bet I'll find legal advice."

"Oh, that's a good idea," I said, practically through my backdoor.

I taught my classes, worrying the whole time about the upcoming meeting. On the way home, I brushed against a low-hanging branch and screamed, imagining the clown tenant's hand, whatever her name was, grabbing at me.

My husband had dinner on the table and the news on. I wolfed down some potato salad while he sliced the turkey breast with a long sleek carving knife the previous owner had left behind--more like a weapon than an ordinary kitchen utensil. *Tell him*, a voice in my brain said, but another voice interrupted, warning me that after he heard the story, he might act impulsively and set in motion a catastrophe involving lawyers or police or any number of possibilities I couldn't imagine as I scooped out some more potato salad. *Besides, maybe the whole thing will blow over*, I thought. *She may not show up.*

But then a commercial for life insurance came on, and I blurted out that soon, one of our tenants would ring the doorbell. Before he could react, she appeared on our TV screen and I shrieked so loud my husband dropped the carving knife, stabbing his foot. Beneath the photo of the clown, AMBER ALERT was displayed in big letters.

"If you know this woman or have any information about her whereabouts, please call the station. She's kidnapped her child and could be dangerous." The news reporter raised her eyebrows like she knew we were out there harboring information. My husband and I stared at each other, and then we saw a stream of blood running along the floor.

"Let's get to the emergency room," I whispered. I was about to turn off the TV when another picture appeared on the screen, this time of the clown tenant with long black hair next to a taller blonde woman.

"Isn't that the one called Midge?" My husband pointed to the tall woman. Then, the same news reporter returned, squinting, like she'd lost us.

"If you encounter this woman who goes by Nancy Hawks and her accomplice Midge, call 911. I grabbed the car keys.

"I'll call your brother and the police along the way and explain everything. It all makes perfect sense," I said.

THE MORNING AFTER CHRISTMAS

I was in the kitchen the morning after Christmas when scads of long gray hair rushed back and forth outside the window, and a big fist pounded on the door.

"Who's that?" my son asked, and I considered throwing the stupid little batteries I'd been trying to wedge into his new Game Boy.

"Here," I said, dropping the toy into his outstretched hands. "You try."

On the way to the door, I got caught up in some wrapping paper and ribbons. My heart pounded in sync with the knocker, whose wild gray hair was a giveaway. It had to be Dad, but I couldn't imagine how he got to Providence. Traveling for Dad consisted of a table covered in maps, his thick finger tracing red lines that might be black on another edition of the same map. Cross-referencing route numbers often led to confusion. You could be swallowed up, trapped God knows where, all because of a colossal goof up. More maps, and we had a ton, did almost nothing to gain his trust in some anonymous distiller of one's whereabouts.

Fear of uncertainty is hard to explain, but it's in our genes; it can't be a coincidence that we're both stuck imagining a range of horrors in the everyday world while others go about their business.

"It's just a door," I've said a million times under my breath, in my mind, or even out loud as I've struggled to take my turn in a revolving door that's about to suffocate me in a malfunctioning state of permanent arrest.

My husband's voice piped up in my brain, wondering why Dad hadn't called. Hadn't called to say he was coming to visit, stay for a while.

"He can't do that," I whispered as I kicked at the wrapping paper.

"Who can't?" my son asked, his eyes glued to the small screen of his new electronic device.

The knocking grew frantic as I told my husband, whose calm brown eyes stood out in my brain, that Dad can't call-- not knowing what I'd say. Would I remember to repeat word for word what comes out of his mouth? A simple reassurance as his life seeped into mine that we were in this together, that I'd never let him disintegrate alone.

"I've got you; I've got you," I said in my heart when he stalled on a bridge on the way to an interview. At five, along for support, I wasn't much help to a news reporter sobbing over the steering wheel.

My husband's confused face faded as I stared at my hand reaching for the gold knob. The moment of contact upon me: "Knob, turn, open," I said, reminding myself that you're always a beginner at staying in the moment, fighting off threatening thoughts that are dying to sprout wings and fly around your brain. I felt the knob's pressure and told myself that it was no more than a fixture from Home Depot, reminiscent of nothing.

"Keep up your guard; stick with the plan you've formulated over the years of adulthood to stave off fear and self-torture," I said, echoing the therapist who sat in my brain with wide, unblinking eyes. Hadn't I counted leaves as I pushed a baby carriage along the streets of Providence, each number helping me tamp down swirling thoughts of fear and its accomplice, guilt? Five thousand leaves before I rid my mind of a memory of me rushing past a woman in the Boston subway. Had I wounded her when our arms touched?

"Go upstairs," I whispered to my son. "You can play better there." Luckily, the screen tricked him into wandering off without argument, out of a contagious area, like this affliction of threatening thoughts is catching, this disease of not believing your hand is actually your hand or a road just a strip of asphalt and not something about to disappear. Besides, somewhere inside, I wanted Dad to myself. In some sick way, I wanted to get back to the disease in its pure form, escape for at least this afternoon, a dull life of recovery.

I opened the door and reminded myself not to mention anything about staying for a while or anything else that might sow seeds of fear, like could he wait a second for me to get a coat, find my hat? *He's here*, I said to myself, and I'd fight the urge to reform him like he should be me, boring but able to get to Pawtucket.

"Dad! How'd you get here?" He put one foot over the threshold and froze before jerking his whole body inside the kitchen. His breathing quickened, like this was the enclosure he'd worried over, envisioned as a windowless prison with us as jailers.

"Drove. Left Muncie at the crack of dawn. Geeze, it's been tough, but I'm managing."

"You're managing," I said, repeating his words like I did as a kid.

"Yeah, women love me," he said. "But I'm particular. Did I tell you about Rose? The one I met at the library?" Instead of this gray-bearded man with wrinkles and hair to his shoulders, I saw the younger version wandering our house on Muncie Avenue, naked, his large penis a wonder to me, his jet black hair greased into a helmet. Even then I knew we had to flaunt the few gifts we could count on. In those moments, he was Alexander the Great, the guy we studied in Latin, a person who feared nothing, whose thoughts weren't a torturous blend of guilt and worry and inexplicable fear.

"This Rose, oh, she's earthy," he said, like he'd forgotten I wasn't some guy at the OTB. "California gal. Wears bracelets and big earrings. Geeze, this is so obscene, I haven't told anyone this." I glanced at the door, praying my son wasn't listening but too afraid to leave Dad for fear he'd vanish if I turned my back.

"Well, Rose calls me up and says, 'Woody, please come over tonight,' and I say, 'all right Rose, but what for?' She says, 'oh come, Woody, pleeze.' Well, I ring the bell, and there's Rose in a flimsy little see-through top and nothing else--god, she's earthy. 'Come in and lie down, Woody,' she says. She's got a bed all made up in the living room, roses in a vase and some kind of drum music going. 'Get bare naked, Woody,' she says, 'and I'll be right back.'Well, I get my clothes off and she comes back with high heels and a whip and a lot of belts strapped around her naked body. 'Wait a minute, Rose,' I say. 'This won't hurt, Woody.'"

"Oh fantastic," I said, my face heating as I swallowed hard, having forgotten how the smallness of his world made it a safe place to be outrageous. No ramifications for Dad in the cage he occupied. Give him a break, I often said to my husband, who hated the braggadocio, disingenuousness of Dad's big talk. Could you survive a life with the absence of real connection, the absence of life beyond a skull full of bombarding terrifying thoughts, I asked. Thank God, he had a seminar and wasn't around to hear this.

Then Dad began to describe being stroked with a thin, sharp whip, interrupting himself with a glance out the window.

"I've gotta go somewhere," he said, and I remembered the day I caught him with his arm around a secretary at the racetrack. A place he managed to get to after hundreds of failed attempts. A place to which he dragged me one Saturday night after Mom, his crutch, went into the hospital. "Gotta go."

You've just arrived, I wanted to say but instead raised my eyebrows. Should I beg him to stay, hang out with his grandson, have a meal with us? But even a moment he can't predict is like jumping off a cliff or slipping between some rocks and no one has the slightest idea of where you are.

"There's someone down at . . . " Dad got a paper out of a pant pocket, held it high so I could see his big scrawl. "Ah bahn pain," he said, warning me as he always did that foreign words, like women with short hair and houses painted colors other than white, should be outlawed. Different was for him alone.

"Au Bon Pain? On Thayer Street? Who?"

"Well, a gal. But the thing is, she's too afraid to meet you. So I left her down there with a book. Hey, she loves to read." I nodded like we were the old team of two off to the carwash on Sunday morning where we met his bookie behind the big hoses. Dad talked to me as we drove about guys he'd like to be--Cassius Clay, anyone brutal. Talked to me like I wasn't a kid but someone who needed to learn about important people. People who had real lives we could pretend were ours for a while.

"Can you babysit? It is kind of an emergency." I had the neighbor girl on the phone as Dad slipped outside, unable, as always, to wait through even a moment of hesitation--a time during which, no matter how quick, he feared his own destruction by an attack of thoughts. They don't hesitate, after all, the thoughts I'd often begged to go away. I'd seen him do the same from the bed he lay in for my middle school years. A bed he didn't leave for a year. I once found a note by his pillow that said *thoughts aren't real.*

"Popsicles are okay, and he can play with his new Game Boy." I yelled to the sitter as I pulled on a jacket and tore out the door.

"Let's get a plan going," Dad said at the helm of his big black Cadillac. We drove toward Au Bon Pain, my palms sweating and Dad breathing hard.

"Can we go back?" I asked. His fear of uncertainty was rubbing off like it usually did. *This is Providence*, I told myself as my stomach flipped up and down. It relaxed when we passed the sign that said DOWNTOWN PROVIDENCE NEXT LEFT.

"You could go in and meet her," he said, ignoring my plea to go back, give up this subterfuge. His eyes gleamed, and I knew I was just part of a plan to do something big and dangerous, live a wild moment or two.

"Sure, sure," I said, as Thayer Street began to tilt one way and then other, like we were on the Tilt-A-Whirl and not on a familiar street near my house.

"But don't tell her who you are. Just mosey up and chat. She's got dark frizzy hair. She'll say I betrayed her if I just go in and say, 'hey, I'd like you to meet my daughter.' We'll drive in silence up to three hours; she'll make me suffer. You go in and find her. You can do that. Can't you?"

"Well, okay. I can do that." He jerked the car into a parking space and jumped out. I raced after him, remembering that he hated to park near a destination, the long walk between the car and the door he'd throw open like an outlaw busting into a saloon a time for self-talk and promotion. The half walk, half run, a time to rehearse speeches the inferiors he was about to encounter needed to hear, that is if he could let the door close behind him and be some place other than his house or the outdoors; that is if he could believe the place wasn't a trap, a coffin for the still-living.

"That's it, that's it. I'll circle it on foot!" He spit as he pointed at Au Bon Pain's yellow sign, and my stomach flip-flopped again at the unnecessary deviousness that fueled his imagined world. He slipped into an alley next to the restaurant and shooed me on. "Can't you handle it? I thought you could do it. Heck, she's scared, sitting somewhere all alone sipping some coffee."

"What's her name?" I backed up, staring at him like he'd leave the minute I went into the restaurant, the minute I took my eyes off him.

"Sometimes Anna," he said, waving me off.

I scanned the tables and circled the restaurant. I even checked the bathroom, but no frizzy brown hair. No woman alone except for the cashier. Maybe whatever her name was had found another ride to wherever. Would Dad stay with me? For a minute, I was hopeful about blending my worlds. Maybe I'd get him to tell all the stories he made up when I was little.

Outside, the alley was empty. I ran from one end to the other, imagining him dead from nervous exhaustion or perhaps he panicked at the newness of it all.

"Dad. Dad. Dad, where are you? Where'd you go?" A guy balancing a pizza box chuckled, and I felt like socking him.

I ran back up Thayer, sometimes dodging people on the sidewalk and then in the street, facing the traffic, searching for Dad's car. At Hope Street, I could barely breathe but kept going, scanning the busier street for the car. Then, like I'd won the lottery, the frizzy brown hair materialized in the passenger seat of the black Cadillac with Indiana plates. I screamed as the car turned on Olney, heading, I suspected, for ninety-five south.

Didn't he know that I'd play along with his version of life in the past, the version I bet he told her? Didn't he know I would've worked with him? Would never goof up his version with one hewing to the tragedy of our fearful lives? *I hate facts,* I wanted to yell. He probably saw me dragging him down, like a drowning person. The lifesaving teacher said, I remember, sitting on the dock at Devil's Lake, that you never know what to expect from a drowning person. They'll pull you right down. And as the leaves and branches rushed back and forth like Dad's hair, I squeezed my eyes shut and then, wide-eyed, ran all the way home.

THE DANCE STUDIO

Bach's French Suite ended, and I took it as a sign to move on.

"Let's wave to the planets." I flopped back and flipped my toes to the ceiling. The kids sat squeezing the soles of their feet together as they flapped their knees. "C'mon, guys; you can't be a butterfly forever!" I hadn't taught kids long, but in just a few weeks, I'd learned not to linger even on a favorite like the butterfly stretch. "Hi, Venus," I called out, pointing and flexing my feet as I searched my brain for the names of planets. "Hi, Pluto--the coldest planet!" I admired my memory as I waved my feet at the cracked ceiling.

"Pluto isn't a regular planet--it's a dwarf planet," Lily said, a regular in Tuesday's Creative Movement class. Dylan smiled at Lily as the group stuck their legs into the air, leaving earth and the gardens we'd been pollinating for the sky. Then Dylan frowned.

"I'm wet."

"Uh-oh." Lily pointed to an expanding puddle.

"Can I put my feet down?" Dylan asked. I hurried to the other side of the room.

"Let's have dance class here today." Dylan crawled away, and Lily held her nose, walking like a young giraffe on her toes.

I had no desire to run a dance studio. I wanted to be a famous dancer or choreographer. When neither of those panned out, I moved from NYC to a town on Long Island where I put an advertisement in the local paper announcing my new career. The idea came to me the moment I finished a memoir about a dancer's last season at the New York City Ballet when she realized she'd never advance beyond the corps. Couldn't I do for the dance studio what she'd done for a dance company--reveal its arcane rules and oddities? Like her, I'd come to a dead end. Oddly, I thought little about the details of running a business.

In August, I found an apartment in a town I knew from weekend trips to its beach. Before even getting my spices in the rack, I headed to the village, searching for a big room where I'd offer kids' dance classes.

"Don't bother with the sale at the church downtown," advised a woman at the mailboxes. "Straight out of a horror film." She pointed to a drooping plant. "Some weird lady forced this on me."

"Horror film?" I imagined starring as a possessed dance teacher.

"Our Lady of Glory," the woman said, placing the half dead plant on a shelf behind a stack of old mail. In a second, I had the church secretary on the phone.

"When can you come?" She inhaled so deeply it sounded like she was sucking the receiver down her throat.

"Now?"

"Bring your checkbook."

When the doorknob fell off, I pounded on the church's red door and waited for what seemed like an hour. *Kids won't be so patient*, I thought, and it dawned on me that I'd never taught kids before. I had never even babysat.

"C'mon!" A woman waved me to another entrance. I'd barely gotten my scarf inside when the door slammed shut and the claustrophobia I didn't know I had kicked in.

I squinted through hazy light at junk here and there.

"Is this it?"

"No, you're in St. Peter's--can't you tell?"

"Love pancakes!" I pointed to a sign for a pancake supper.

"You missed it--that was a year ago. I hope you remembered your checkbook." The glow from her cigarette guided us to a small smoke-filled office with a blaring CB radio. "Can you leave a few months' rent?" She slammed the door and a small pot tipped over, scattering tacks across the filthy carpet. Unable to move, I tossed her the check, and she tossed me a bag of barbecue potato chips she'd fished from a wastebasket. "Like a receipt."

On the first day, I arrived all of five minutes before class-- half because I never wanted to go into the spooky church again, and half because I was busy writing a producer in New York about a new dance drama I hoped might catch his attention.

As some kids filed in, followed by mothers and a bemused father, I rushed to move a trike and a scooter. Two girls beat me to the trike and a boy in cowboy boots screamed after the scooter fell, pinning him under the handle.

"They wouldn't let me move anything beforehand," I lied to a scowling parent.

Enrollment grew slowly, giving me time to plot my next move. I kept the diary but only half-heartedly. Basically, I liked the steady flow of cash. It reminded me of waitressing in Midtown, where I'd rush from the restaurant to an audition with the pockets of my red apron full of coins. As if they were leaving a tip, the parents paid for one or two classes at a time. I liked the quick reward. I also liked running in, devising a quick combination of movement, or spontaneously coming up with a cool improvisation. Seeing the kids imitate my movements spurred me on. Time flew by.

A vague foreboding hung over the studio, but the rush of being in charge of my dancing life, unlike waiting for a phone call, blinded me to warning signs. A parent slipped on the ice one afternoon as she dragged her kid along the decrepit sidewalk, and when she finally coerced the kid into class, she jokingly muttered that she would never sue such a nice person.

The lights flickered, and one day we danced in the dark. Another day, one of the portable barres I'd made out of sawhorses and old broom handles toppled onto a girl's leg. A spot of blood leaked through her pink tights. "A bad sign," she whispered.

I never saw the secretary, although I heard the radio blaring from her office. One afternoon, a girl asked to use the bathroom and ran back sobbing.

"A lady in the bathroom said she'd bite me!" The possibility of crazy people roaming the cavernous church hadn't crossed my mind. Other than the secretary, of course.

I raced to the bathroom, the class dissolving into bedlam. A woman in a long fur coat and a tiara stood guard at the door.

"Tell those devils to stay away!" She pushed me into a wall before fleeing into the church. Later, as I locked up, the secretary phoned, warning me to control my students. I nodded, thinking I should rent a new place.

Gradually, however, the secretary and the bathroom lady seemed more phantom than real. My music blocked out the CB radio for the most part, and the next time I encountered the bathroom lady, she offered me a half-eaten donut and admitted to loving my father.

Before I knew it, I began to look forward to teaching, especially the Creative Movement class. I even began planning the class. We were mountains, lions, gorillas, snowbanks, fairies, sprites, clouds--anything that popped into my mind or theirs. One girl insisted on wearing patent leather shoes, another a cape, someone else sunglasses, and this was okay; unlike ballet, the uniform wasn't important. By the time the ballet students arrived, I'd delved so far into the world of non-technical movement that the clear-cut, pristine world of ballet reminded me of a crisp salad after the swirling textures of a full meal. I switched gears, clapping my hands like a Russian teacher I'd studied with as a kid. Before I knew it, the day was over, and I was too exhausted to dream up plans beyond heating up a can of soup.

But one afternoon, it all changed--at least for a good twenty minutes. I left the house later than usual, having worked until the last minute on a proposal for a performance piece about running a dance studio--like a precursor to the book I'd mostly forgotten about. Unfortunately, my beat-up car had a flat. I grabbed my dance bag and sprinted to the studio, where skeptical parents listened to my excuse as I exaggerated my breathing, practically gasping.

The kids were settled into the stretching routine, when out of the blue, a shy boy named Sam rolled on Henry.

"Henry hit me!" Sam and Henry began to chase each other, and the whole class joined in. A new girl galloped to the front, and everyone galloped behind.

"Great!" I smiled at the little band, moving in a clump. But Henry ran in front of this girl who cared more about perfecting the gallop than being first. "Okay, running is fine," I said, not really meaning it. Henry pivoted, whacking Sam, and the whole group collapsed domino-style. A girl who'd been saddled with three last names rubbed her elbow.

"Are you all right, Taylor?" Luckily, Taylor popped up, and I made her a leader. "Everyone get behind Taylor for skips."

"I'm never a leader," Sophie frowned.

"Okay--two lines."

We skipped the length of the room a couple times.

"Let's be skipping swans!" I slipped the Saint-Saens CD into the boom box, searching for a favorite, "The Dying Swan."

We skipped, galloped, and leapt over imaginary puddles. Too bad Isadora Duncan had already made simple traveling steps to great classical music a subversive act because, at that moment, I knew my calling: leading young kids in lines of locomotion. There simply had to be some way of turning this exhilaration into something noteworthy. *Isadora was lucky,* I thought, daydreaming. Not the scarf and the wheel, of course, and then there was the matter of her children drowning. But everything else.

"Hey, what's wrong with Henry?" I turned around to find Taylor hovering over a motionless Henry. The rest of the kids backed into me.

"Henry!" I yelled, worrying that one of Isadora's dead kids had come back through Henry. "Henry!"

"Henry won't get up," Sam said, shaking his head. I fell to Henry's side. His eyes rolled upward, and foam dribbled from his half-open mouth.

"Oh, Henry!" I stared at his stony face as the hairs on my arms stood up.

"Did you see Henry fall?" I asked the huddle of speechless kids. "Did *anyone* see Henry fall or hit his head on the floor or maybe the radiator?" We all turned to the radiator spewing steam and hot water.

"We don't dance by the radiator," Sophie said. "You said it's a rule."

"I know, I know." I stared at Henry, who lay still except for the bubbles that continued to collect on his chin. *At least I'd established a few safety rules*, I thought as my hand waivered above Henry's forehead, too afraid to actually touch any part of his stiffening corpse.

Every bit of information I'd never fully understood about dealing with corpses or the seriously injured (culled mainly from hospital dramas) swirled about in my brain: don't move the neck, lift the eyelids and shine a small flashlight into the eyes, and put a popsicle stick in the mouth or perhaps blow in the mouth while pinching the nose or pump the chest with your fists. Or was it your palms? Basically, I did nothing but stare at Henry, who'd obviously suffered a head injury and was now in a coma. His skin took on a blue color, and I noticed his fingers were incredibly straight and stiff. As his skin turned from blue to gray, I thought of the midday sky and wished I'd seen it as a warning. I could see the email I should have sent: "Classes called off due to foreshadowing of negligence."

My brain switched gears, realizing I could go to prison. I pictured myself leading dance classes in windowless recreation rooms with armed guards at the doors. Prisoners are especially tough on people who do terrible things to children. Ten years for reckless skipping leading to a child in a vegetative state-- solitary confinement would be the only solution. *For how long*, I'd ask the sneering guard. *Indefinitely*, she would say, and then I realized that this guard was the church secretary.

"Shouldn't you call an ambulance?" Sophie brought me back to reality. I grabbed my cell phone from the pocket of my jacket, realizing I'd never collected parents' phone numbers.

"Do any of you know Henry's phone number or last name?" The kids looked puzzled.

"I live at thirteen forty-five Freeman Way," a kid said. The 911 operator would probably ask for Henry's last name and perhaps his phone number or his parents' information, at the very least. The judge would add a good five years for dangerous and reckless administration of a dance studio.

911 flashed across my cell. What would I remember from these last moments of freedom--images of Henry's stiff body, foaming mouth, and frozen gaze?

"I'd like to report a child in a coma from skipping and falling in my dance studio."

"Is he dead?" Sam asked.

"My grandma died," Taylor said. The 911 operator asked if I had administered first-aid. I didn't even have a box of Band-Aids. The judge in the case would want a list of first-aid equipment I kept on hand. She'd want to see a diploma for a first-aid course. Lawyers would close briefcases as I wept. They might try to convince the judge, who probably had endured a sadistic ballet teacher, that I lost the diploma or that the schizophrenic bathroom dweller had stolen my first-aid supplies.

I could only wait now for men and women in blue to storm through the door, shackle me and, worse, toss me into the caged backseat of an overheated car whose back seat locks were in a locked down position.

"Please, Henry, please." I knelt over Henry. *Wake up little Susie, wake up!* The oldies lyrics taunted me. No more oldies, no more dancing in my small kitchen as I dreamed of stardom or at least some kind of success.

"Wake up, little Henry, wake up!" I sobbed, and the kids stared at me, some smiling. Lily clapped. A few joined in and we sang to Henry's comatose body. I pictured us on a Netflix series.

"What's going on, Henry?" An exasperated voice came from nowhere. Had I begun to hear voices? "Henry--what are you doing?" We stopped singing as high heels clicked across the floor.

Henry's mother, in a long black coat, stood at Henry's feet.

"I am really sorry. He's been doing this fake death thing at school. Okay, Henry, enough already. I've had it, Henry!"

"Move away!" A 911 woman stormed through the door. Her partner followed. "Give us room, give us room!" Henry's mother plucked a grinning Henry from the floor.

"No computer time for you!" Henry's mother eyed the 911 woman as she flashed her light around the room, searching for whatever caused a death that never happened. I worried that I'd be called before a judge for wasting the time of emergency workers who should be saving real dying people. But mostly I tried to get my heart to stop pounding.

"So everything's fine here?" The woman turned off her flashlight and clapped her hands on her guns that extended far from her hips, reminding me of the *panniers* I'd worn in a Baroque opera back in college. *I could choreograph an opera about 911 workers*, I thought--*something having to do with gun control or a post-9/11 obsession with first responders*. My heart slowed down, my mind full of costume ideas.

"Yes, everything is fine--everything is perfect." Then, as if I needed another inspiration, another performance idea to chase, in rushed the bathroom-dwelling woman dressed in a sky blue formal gown, followed by the secretary.

"Don't shoot," the woman begged. "Please don't shoot," she wailed.

"She stole my chips, and this isn't the first time." The secretary pointed her cigarette at the crazy woman and held up a bag of chips. "The radio said you were coming, and let me tell you, it's about time." Most parents took this as a cue to leave.

"We will take off." The 911 woman gave the room another once over as her co-worker listened to a call for help.

"Can I show you my leap?" Sophie and her mom hung back.

"Sophie loves your class. I wonder if she should move up?" Sophie leaped around the edge of the room as we followed her progress.

"She should stay here; she's a leader." Sophie grabbed my hand, and we leapt as her mother silenced her cell phone. After she dropped the phone into her leather bag, she smiled and raised her eyebrows.

"I've been meaning to ask if I could help you--with, you know, making this more like a real dance studio?"

Sophie grabbed my hand, and I joined her, relieved to leave her mother and a discussion perhaps about the dance studio's future, one full of unwavering ideas and consistent goals.

"Can you come to my house?" Sophie asked as we stopped dancing. I shook my head and looked back at her mother.

"I can't, Sophie. I need to buy a first-aid kit at the drug store."

THE SPIDER BITE

The spider bite yanked me out of a nightmare in which I was being tortured in a windowless basement by an excruciating disco beat and a single overhead light bulb. Panting, I squinted at the sun seeping through the mini blinds, relieved to have escaped a minimalist nightmare probably meant to warn me about jogging exclusively to "Stayin' Alive."

"Rigidity leads to depression," a therapist I dated had warned. I closed my eyes, wondering if it also leads to a throbbing hand.

At first, I scoffed at the pulsing white pearl cradled in the webbing between my ring and pinky fingers. But then my racing heart reminded me of my dermatologist informing me that small is often worse than big.

"You probably dismissed this seemingly insignificant mole on your shoulder," he'd whispered in my ear.

I brushed off the memory of the man's hot breath and remembered how cold and uncomfortable I'd been at a party the night before, sitting on a pile of splintery logs in suburban Rhode Island. As I wiggled the pimple, it dawned on me that I'd probably been bitten by a displaced log dweller.

I raced to the computer, tripping over a laundry basket I'd deposited in the hallway. As I rubbed my shin and hopped over a pile of tax documents, I vowed to curb an obsession with obstacle courses. Tidiness would be key to eliminating whatever the computer decided I had.

Following Google's orders, I closely examined the pimple, finding two side-by-side bite marks. According to Google, the placement of this double bite--between fingers or toes--indicates the biter was a brown recluse spider.

"Prefers enclosed spaces, lives in wood piles, and usually bites at twilight." It then warned the weak in bold letters not to click on pictures. I logged off and relived the scene on the woodpile, surrounded by shivering cocktail drinkers.

"Oh, it's you." An immaculately coiffed woman I recognized from my neighborhood caught me tugging on a hair sprouting from my chin.

"Oh, hi," I said, quickly placing my hand on the woodpile like I was at home on my couch. She gave a quick nod and looked past me as she launched into a longish story about turning her neighbors into city officials for lapses in home maintenance. I wondered if she knew that parties provide many of the stories I incorporate into my performance art.

"The city serves citations, and that gets these slobs motivated," she said, sipping some white wine. "At first, I left anonymous notes--the kind that would make me paranoid, but that didn't work." She shook her head, dismayed at the strength of peoples' psyches.

Rather than reprimand her for policing the neighborhood, I nodded--a fool-proof method for encouraging confessions.

But this time, my deviousness went too far, as I said nothing when she described her first foray into neighborhood policing, a bumbling episode that caused the death, I realized, of my friend's cat.

"Finally, I don't have to listen to its sobbing." She drained her wine before wiping the rim with her napkin. "Great talking." She turned away to greet a man biting into a stuffed date.

I'm not crazy enough to believe my tacit approval of her vigilantism caused the spider to bite me or so deranged to think the spider would have spared me if I'd reprimanded this woman for dropping a ladder on a cat. The bite wasn't direct punishment, but had I jumped up in repulsion, I might have shaken off the spider. Instead, I nodded and sipped like it was okay to secretly police her neighborhood.

Clearly, this habit of usurping stories was taking its toll. On day two, I woke to a pounding heart and hand, as well as a little voice informing me that the poison was spreading throughout my body.

"That's what happens," the voice said and then disappeared as I begged for more explanation. I stayed in bed, wondering if a scolding call to this woman would shrink the fiery red infection expanding across my palm.

Wasn't I practically coercing information from people? I envisioned myself imprisoned for the act of tricking. Or was I guilty of something, like not helping a blind person across the street? Perhaps if I'd admonished this anal-retentive woman, she'd have at least apologized to my friend whose sobbing voice now haunted me. Then, one of my molars began to throb, and I experienced a surge of panic. Soon, I'd be paralyzed for causing the death of my friend's cat.

"That's absurd!" I tried to get out of bed just to show how completely unparalyzed I was and how ridiculous my thoughts were becoming. Instead, I fell back, aware of a numbness settling in over the right side of my body.

On day three, I woke to a new patch of black skin. Panting, I ran to the bathroom, banging my toe into a stack of books I'd forgotten to shelve. With a throbbing toe and hand, I filled the tub--soaking being better than a doctor questioning my sanity, giving me mind-altering drugs, and perhaps shoving me into an MRI. As I stepped into the tub, a squirrel clung to the window, his beady eyes warning me, and I decided to get outside and away from my house.

In blinding midsummer light, I circled the block picturing life on the streets. *This stupid bug bite would be trivial to a homeless person*, I thought as I passed a woman asleep at the bus stop. Sweat dripped into my eyes as my teeth chattered. I'd remember to bring her a blanket when this ordeal was over.

My neighborhood stumbling propelled me closer to the nearby hospital. After I triggered the automatic door to the emergency room a million times, a nurse in sickening colors emerged.

"We're worried the door's gonna break," she said, pointing me toward the overflowing waiting room decorated with suspended televisions and paintings of flowers and sunsets.

"I'm coming in, but I'm fairly positive I left the oven on," I said, eyeing a metal door with the sign: DON'T ENTER RADIOACTIVE MATERIALS.

"If you're looking for drugs, you're barking up the wrong tree." The nurse rolled her eyes, her smirk pushing me to the stratosphere of anxiety.

"Please forgive me," I pleaded, as I imagined striking her with a hot poker and then being hauled off to the room with radioactive materials. I backed up and rammed into a doctor.

"How long has it been like this?" The doctor placed my hand in her palm like it was a glove she'd found on the street.

Like what? I screamed silently as I followed her inside. After locating me in the computer, she handed me a prescription for antibiotics and a warning:

"If it gets worse, you'll be admitted."

Never preface bad news! I shouted inside my head as I stared at a poor man hobbling by with a twisted foot. The doctor smiled just as a giant black bird crowed on one of the suspended TV sets. I thought of Peter denying Christ the third time. *I should've gone to medical school*, I thought, *just so I'd know everything before it happened or could happen.*

I hurried out of the waiting room, skirting a woman cradling a finger wrapped in tinfoil.

The punishments had only begun for sins, stemming from the death of my friend's cat. The worst of my sins, I decided, was being as devious as Iago, faking empathy for my friend but in reality, hating animals, especially cats. The woman with the white wine was simply the messenger, informing me of the depth of my complicity. Sure enough, the next day I woke panting and exhausted from being chased by a group of young residents through a never-ending hospital ward. When I found my hand, I could plainly see that it wasn't just worse, it was dying. The blackish hue, now in full force, crept over the retracting, lizard-like skin and the knob had become quite squishy but still impenetrable.

Then the phone rang.

Tangled in the sheets, I couldn't get to the phone, but I heard the message:

"Hi, Mom. There's been some bombs in London, and I just wanted you to know that I'm all right." Unable to disentangle myself, I hobbled to the phone, taking the sheets with me.

"Don't hang up!" I screamed at the machine. Her phone in London couldn't accept incoming calls. If only I could talk to her and not just the blinking answering machine, I'd reassure myself that she needed me and therefore I couldn't die, couldn't succumb to this out-of-the-blue assault on my health and sanity.

I could, however, succumb to the cold. It may have been about ninety degrees, but my teeth chattered, and my panicking thoughts told me that my daughter's life had been spared and that mine would be taken. How I wished that my daughter's father had been more than sperm I'd bought. She's so unneurotic that I bet the sperm owner would've helped me out of this quagmire--perhaps by marrying me. Like her, he'd think logically--our marriage would be best for all.

But in the meantime, I had to get outside. Complete dressing was unimportant. My house had morphed into a quickly draining hourglass. No one dies outside, with the exception of all Jack London characters. I threw a raincoat over my nightgown, slipped into combat boots, and headed to the bakery around the corner, my hand wrapped in an ace bandage. I hadn't eaten in what had to be a long time.

There I saw the headline on the front page of The New York Times: OVER SLEPT? YOU LIVED. CAUGHT THE BUS? YOU DIED. Beneath this headline were photos of blood smattered Londoners, some stumbling, some obviously dead on the sidewalk.

I felt my knees buckle, picturing my daughter alive amidst the carnage. As a family, we'd used up our year's worth of extraordinary luck. I peeked under the bandage, praying that the red army racing across my hand and the blackish green skin left in its wake had all disappeared, but if anything, the army was charging ahead, wrapping swiftly around my hand so the skin was either bright red or sickeningly dark and mutilated.

Perhaps it was the color photo of blood-stained Londoners mixed with the vivid deterioration of my poor skin that brought me to a halt. Maybe the constant pulse between my fingers brought on something like a stroke. As I slumped onto a tree stump by the bakery, my eyes glazed over, and my ears rang. Could this be the beginning of a sacrifice rite, exchanging my life for my daughter's?

"Didn't I see you? Earlier in the week, maybe?" The same doctor had one foot on the tree stump like she was about to begin a Swedish exercise routine. "How's the hand, anyway? Ready for amputation?"

My exhausted mind and body refused to recoil from her strange sense of humor, and I held up my hand.

"Let's hope not. Have you been taking the antibiotics?" I shook my head, sensing that this long transition to death, the prologue to an intractable moment of reckoning I feared more than death itself, had come to an end.

"You really need to come in. She stared at the pimple, spreading my fingers carefully. "I want to lance that." I jumped to my feet.

"Will lancing cure it?" My brain was suddenly cleansed of its vast inventory of anxieties. Yes, I was a bad person on so many counts, but I could start over as a nun but without taking official orders. She ignored the question, still pushing the pimple around.

"We better get started. That looks really painful, and if reconstruction is necessary. . . well, let's wait for the plastic surgeon." She said nothing about the antibiotic drip. Just the magic word: lancing. I have no problem with piercing, probing, pinching--even whacking. There is nothing mysterious about teeth drilling, for instance--nothing to make one wonder about the consequences of ingesting unknown ingredients. Back at the hospital, behind the turquoise curtain, she stabbed the pimple with a vicious instrument.

As the spider's poison dripped down my fingers, I fell asleep, half waking to hear the plastic surgeon confide in the doctor. Forgetting my resolve to never again steal another story, I strained to hear him through the curtain.

"Had a patient yesterday with the exact same bite," he said. "Hate to say anyone deserves one of these gruesome looking things, but this woman said she got bit climbing a tree in her backyard. Does this all the time to get good photos of her neighbor's rotting gutters, peeling paint--things like that. Sends the photos to the housing authority! Can you believe it? She's like some sheriff of home improvement. Thank god she doesn't live in my neighborhood."

As the bag of liquid antibiotics began to slowly empty itself into my arm, I resisted asking the nurse if the bag contained a mixture of cyanide and LSD. Then I heard the doctors whispering in loud voices.

"Do you think either of these bug bite victims is looking at reconstruction?"

"Not sure," the plastic surgeon laughed. "But if I had to bet, I'd say Miss Vigilante will most likely lose part of her hand. I think her spider used a lot more poison.

RHYTHMIC TOUR GUIDE FOR CHILDREN

I managed to snap apart the plastic chopsticks without making a sound. Then, with uncharacteristic skill, I pinched a single chunk of General Tsao Chicken, extracting it with care from a mound too big for one person. *They'll box up the leftovers. Think of it as tomorrow's lunch,* a voice in my head advised. *Okay, but please no Styrofoam,* I begged. The squeaking stays in my head for days.

On the other side of the beige Formica table and wedged into a scarred wooden highchair, a baby verging on not being a baby anymore tried to grab the glossy square of meat that hung from the tips of my chopsticks like a guy in a cherry picker. I jerked my chair backward, retreating as he barked little attacking sounds and chugged his highchair forward, kicking his thick legs straight out and in as if he were pumping a swing. With nowhere to go, he flopped back and stuck a fist in his mouth.

With only four of us in the restaurant, I couldn't figure out why the waitress stuck me in a corner across from this fleshy child and an emaciated woman wearing a tee shirt with the words "mother or smother" printed in psychedelic pink--perhaps a translation error.

I smiled at the kid, pretending I thought him adorable, when really I wanted to catch the woman's eye, send her a telepathic message to stop wolfing down her rice. Her churning and gulping were turning my stomach.

"Ooh, ooh," the kid gurgled in a friendly tone as he waved a clump of noodles back and forth. I widened my fake smile as I waved my piece of chicken in synch with his noodles--two silent metronomes.

You can teach rhythm with anything, I thought, imagining myself leading a group of kids skipping along an alley somewhere in China--there were pagodas mixed with office towers in the background, so maybe Beijing. I really want to go to Asia, and I really want to stop teaching ballet. I'd read retirees should never jettison a career's worth of skills when searching for something to do before they die. Rhythmic Tour Guide for Children fit the bill better, I guess, than scriptwriter for a stay-at-home travel series--a recent fixation. I love daydreaming about new jobs and trips, which is weird since I can barely get from Providence to East Providence due to my agoraphobia.

Without warning, the baby screamed and began to wildly swing his noodles back and forth in a perfect imitation of branches tossed about in a flash storm. For a moment I wondered if he somehow knew that choreographic transitions had fallen out of favor. I was about to follow suit--being a devotee of the quick change from slow to fast or the opposite-

-by popping the lilting piece of meat into my mouth, when the ceiling in Pawtucket's Taste Delicious Restaurant collapsed. Plates of pale blue-green glass fell, shattering over rows of empty tables. A thick metal rod slammed into my back, missing the kid by an inch.

"Your baby!" I yelled at the woman, flinging the chunk of chicken on to one of her empty plates. Then, fearing that the stranded cube of meat predicted a future when I'd be the only person left on earth, I asked her for the square of meat, but only in my head.

A chunk of glass slid off the woman's head as she slurped the last of a pale brown soup. She sprang up and grabbed the kid, loosening him from the highchair by twisting him side to side like a cork in a bottle. They disappeared through a door I hadn't noticed before, leaving me pinned to my seat, unable to reach the stranded piece of chicken and wondering why the kid hadn't cried during his extraction.

I tried skidding my chair back as pieces of hardware fell and bounced off tables and chairs, but I was stuck under the weight of the bar. A woman with long gray hair, the only other person left in the restaurant, began to scream. When more glass rained down, I matched her scream for scream like this was some kind of contest. It reminded me of my brother and me wailing as Dad whipped the furniture with his belt after we set off his misophonia with our rude eating noises. Instead of beating us, he would whip the furniture, but we screamed anyway. As more glass fell, I imagined him on a rampage in the Taste Delicious Restaurant, overturning one table after the next as the woman who had now disappeared gobbled her food.

At last, the glass stopped falling, the woman with the long gray hair and I stopped screaming, and a giant air conditioning tube uncurled to the floor--a near replica of the fire escape chute attached to the side of my elementary school in East Lansing, Michigan. I hunched forward under the weight of the metal bar, my chin on the table, remembering the janitor's hands reaching for us as we flew down the tube during fire drills, our white underpants practically in his face.

"What should we do?" I called to the lady with the long gray hair, straining to hear an answer as the lights went out.

In the dark, I worried that I might be stuck forever in Pawtucket. *Not in Pawtucket*, I begged while slithering underneath the table, flattening myself like the mice that slip through the narrow, practically invisible cracks in my kitchen floor. *Not in this tawdry city that refused to get cool, resisting art fairs, sidewalk sales, and even a river relocation.*

The lights flashed on and off, warning us of more disaster.

"I'm leaving," I yelled, but still no answer. Then I crawled over the glass strewn floor to the door I prayed hadn't moved or disappeared in what could be the first earthquake in Rhode Island history.

Outside in the freezing air, I hung onto a dumpster, my back on fire and my heart pounding at the thought of going to a hospital. I am not only afraid to travel (getting to Pawtucket is a cinch since I live on the Providence Pawtucket line) but also of drugs. I'd read of a doctor accidentally injecting someone with a hallucinogenic--a type that never wears off. Well, actually, I added the part about it never wearing off. You can see why I avoid science fiction.

From a side door emerged the waitress, the ravenous mother and her baby, a cook, and a young translator, who begged me to come back to the ruined Taste Delicious Restaurant the next day for remedies.

"Come back--we have good medicine," the girl said, braiding her fingers with mine. "We will help you with good drugs," she glanced over her shoulder at the others. They ignored her, talking amongst themselves. I backed up, about to run from the talk of drugs. Were these people mind readers or had the food been laced with a drug that made my brain transparent? No more General Tsao Chicken. Then I remembered I hadn't eaten anything.

"Will we see you?" She grabbed my other hand and pulled me along, the two of us galloping and then skipping past the parking lot and over the cracked sidewalk to a NO PARKING sign we circled. We headed back to the applause of the group. The woman with the long gray hair stepped out of Taste Delicious Restaurant like the clapping was her cue to join us. Without pausing, the young translator grabbed her hand, and the three of us skipped in the opposite direction, toward a boarded up tattoo shop.

When we returned this time, the group joined in, skipping behind us in two rows like a corps de ballet. I called out counts after a third time around or maybe a fourth. I added an arm movement but most struggled to get on the right leg and couldn't manage to add the arm. Finally, we all dropped hands, gasping, and the young translator told me and the gray-haired lady that we needed to pay for our meals, but they'd give us a discount.

CAN I STAY FOR A WHILE?

The thing is, I love these people, Richard and Sally Richardson, old neighbors and salt of the earth. The minute Robin left me or kicked me out, I went straight to these two, but unfortunately they weren't home. I hung out on their porch for a while, surveying the old neighborhood. I think if we'd stayed in this admittedly down-and-out place--stayed put--Robin and I might still be together. I wish in some ways that we'd never uprooted the family and moved to the burbs. It dawned on me sitting alone on Richard and Sally's steps for I don't know how long that Robin reverted to her southern Republican self when we moved to Singleton. Although, she always said the Richardsons were too weird for her, while I just loved 'em. Of course, I'm a people person and totally open-minded.

It was getting dark when I got up to leave, but I could swear I saw Richard in an old pick-up truck back up and then make a quick turn away from his own house! I waved and called his name, but no luck; he was out of earshot. But anyway, I am back a few weeks later, still thinking about the good old days as I pounded on their door. I prayed they were home this time because the motel was getting old and, needless to say, depressing.

Richard answered, and of course I could see that he was psyched to see me. Psyched because we're like-minded.

"Hey, Richard. How are you? I am terrible, miserable, gonna kill myself. But I won't; don't worry. Is Sally home, too? Can I come in and get your advice? Or can I just tell you what it's like when you lose your job and then your wife and kids? Sorry, not funny."

"Hi, Michael," Richard said in his quiet voice. He blinked his eyes a few times like he had a problem with a contact. I don't know if he wears contacts, but he blinked like he might, or maybe he was just trying to get rid of something. Then he looked around, a little confused. That's so Richard. Lost in his own house. "Sally's out, but sure . . . come in. I'm not sure when she'll be home," he said, motioning me inside. "She's rehearsing a dance in the North Burial Ground. We're both, um, so sorry about what's going on," he said, his voice halting in between words. It was so obvious the guy felt really bad for me, and his hesitation was natural. People don't know what to say or can't believe anything like this would happen to me of all people. We stood in the freezing foyer while Richard struggled to close the door. "This door has never really worked," he muttered. "That's why we never use it. But yeah, we're both sorry for you losing the job and then the other thing."

"I know, I know," I said, realizing that my trauma, this fucking undeserved disaster, would unnerve a gentle soul like

Richard. And, of course, my celebrity puts me in a different realm. People saw me every night on television; that is, before I lost my job. I think some even thought I lived in front of the camera in a bubble of importance, which I practically did, and I can't believe that Robin thought I should just move on after I got pushed out.

"Do anything to bring in the bacon," she said, not caring at all about how much I unearthed as a reporter, as someone who gives a damn. But anyway, most people don't get how sensitive and passionate I am, except maybe for these two-- Richard and Sally.

"But Richard, my buddy, I still love Robin." I grabbed his arm as we stood in the small foyer full of junk mail, shoes, and some old umbrellas. "Where did it go wrong, Richard?" I sobbed, tears blinding me for a second. Once I wiped my eyes with a napkin Richard found in one of his pockets, I could see, even though he was back struggling with the doorknob, that he wanted me to get back with Robin. He wanted the best for me and not just because I am a bit of a celebrity. The guy is just such a good egg. "Can I stay for a while?" I asked, knowing that it would be perfectly fine.

"Well, yeah, um, yeah, ah, sure." Richard gave up on the door and nodded in his noble, distracted way. He'd probably been thinking about some tidbit of history, being a history teacher and all. Although now that I think about it, I'm not sure what he teaches.

I shook a few Junior Mints into his palm, and he led me right in. No hesitation on Richard's part, none at all. I almost pointed out that his fingernails were dirty. Instead, I held my hand in the air for a moment, flashing my clean nails. Hopefully, if I stayed long enough, he'd see me as a model. All those years in front of the camera gave me a kind of glow that could rub off on Richard.

"God, it is so good to know that Robin was wrong about you and Sally. You guys are the type of people who care and understand. She got on some kind of business-minded track influenced, I am sure, by her strait-laced family. "I can't even eat," I said, following Richard into their cavernous kitchen.

I remember when they bought this wreck of a place. Richard worked on it all the time. I used to see him on rickety ladders, paintbrush in hand. Robin wondered why they didn't take a loan out and get it done in one fell swoop, but process was never Robin's thing, and it never will be. My sister told me that when I called her sobbing so hard, she offered to come live with me. She told me we were never meant to be--Robin and me--because I am so special.

"Our family just is," she said. "We're poets," she yelled into the phone, and then she read me some lines she'd just written about a dog she'd found frozen. Then she sang the lines. No wonder Robin forbade my sister from visiting ever again. I mean I love her, God knows I do, but after talking with her, actually listening to her for more than a minute or two, your mind is literally flooded with worry and, I guess, doubt, which combined, begets pure aggravation. I hung up as fast as I could. Now, unfortunately, she calls me everyday--except on

Mondays when she sings at some coffee house and has to get prepared.

But Richard and Sally are pure, simple love and acceptance (I may have said that already), which a person like me really appreciates. I guess you'd say I'm too sensitive for the world. I mentioned this to Richard as he handed me a piece of buttered toast on a plate with an enormous chip that led to a crack. I actually wondered if the plate was going to split before I could move some newspapers on their beat up Butcher Block table and set it down.

"Uh huh," Richard said, biting into his toast, which he cradled in one hand while stroking his mustache with the other. The toast unfortunately broke in two and fell to the floor, where I saw a lot of grit. Vague grit, the kind Providence, this dump of a city, specializes in. Anyway, the dog gobbled up the toast before Richard could grab it. "So. . .how's finding a job?" Richard asked, clapping his hands as he swallowed the last bit of burnt toast. I stared at the flecks of toast floating to the old, pitted wood floor.

"I'm an investigative reporter, not a PR guy," I told Richard, who raised his eyebrows and nodded like he implicitly understood what Robin and her passel of Republican idiot brothers didn't understand.

"So, okay, I have been offered a job writing PR for some friend of Robin's brother from his beloved fraternity. A big muckety-muck who runs some kind of fund up in Boston, and I refuse to go that route. I'd personally rather run a wedding video service than join a world where I'd write nothing more than corporate Hallmark card greetings all day." God, I hate those guys who probably bullied Robin into being the way she is now, which is not her in the long run. It's not her. "Richard! How can I get her back?" Richard froze for a moment, cocked his head.

"Is it just the firing--I mean getting laid off--that is the crux of the problem?" he asked as he moved a half-eaten cake with a candle in the shape of a six sagging into the cracked chocolate icing. "Hey, I don't mean to interrupt everything here, but I should try to get down the Christmas tree lights now that it's close to Easter. I think it's close. Actually, I'm not quite sure when Easter is, but I know Sally would love it if I got up on the roof and at least got the reindeer down so she can put up a bunny she made out of dryer lint."

Then Neil, their six-year-old son, walked in without pants on, which could be construed as odd for a six-year-old, but I only registered the kid's oddness for a second before I burst into tears again. Something about this half-naked kid reminded me of my old priest who'd begun calling me everyday, and here I am, not even Catholic anymore. But this guy, just like Richard, is golden and not warped like Robin said he must be. No, I wanted to shout at her, and maybe I did once or twice. The guy is golden, guiding me, speaking to me in the tones of some soft bells that chime and fill my head with the beauty that, thank god, drives out all the words Robin flung at me. Drives 'em straight out; gives 'em the boot. I might call Robin, let her know that her mind is shrink wrapped like a winterized boat, only in her case it's all year long. I'd also tell her for the millionth time that I need to be in front of the camera where I'd been for ten years before this so-called downturn.

I followed Richard upstairs, and so did Neil, who, I gotta say, is one smart kid for his age, but I didn't expect him to know about the notice in the newspaper. I honestly didn't think Richard or Sally would've known about the police deal since police reports are only listed in local papers, and who'd thought they'd read the *Singleton Times*? It's a stupid, silly, suburban rag. "We wondered if you actually hit Canary," Neil said, standing on the top stair like some kind of child Buddha.

"Do you mean Robin?" I asked, feeling tears about to roll as I remembered the whole family, even little Michael, playing a word game of associations that, of course, comes from my family. We have the intellectual bent missing from Robin's family, and she loved our family, loved it, recognized it as, let's say it, superior. "Can you read?" I asked, holding back the tears and dodging junk lining both sides of the wooden staircase. I have to say that our new Singleton pad was so much more organized than these old places, but still, I can't see Richard and Sally and probably me any other place than right here amidst the history and character of these ramshackle houses and windy sidewalks covered in dog shit. Speaking of dog shit, Neil smells, and Richard's white shirt is yellow under his arms and looks like it's had its day as a shirt--more like a rag now.

"We wondered if you really hit her," Neil said, loud this time. "That's what we think it said in the paper," Neil said, circling Richard, who struggled with one of those goddamn windows I hated so much. Getting the storms up alone made me swear a blue streak, but never in front of the children. Sorry, Robin; you're wrong on that count.

Richard didn't seem to hear anything Neil said, probably because he had the reindeer on his mind or maybe the bunny. Our like-mindedness couldn't have been more obvious. Shitty windows, roofs, decorations, wires--God, I hate that stuff and obviously Richard does, too. I knew I should give him a hand, but I hate waiting for directions or standing with some shitty wire I'm supposed to wrap in a neat coil like I'm a fucking Boy Scout. I did give Neil some Junior Mints, not, by the way, to shut him up. Just to be nice to the poor kid whose legs were blue with cold.

"And yes," I blurted, "I didn't hit Robin. I mean, 'no' to your question, Neil."

Richard had a foot out on the roof so he may not have been privy to this little confession, but I had to make my case right then and there. We were in a study, I think, as it had a few bookcases and an old desktop computer on a board held up by two old green filing cabinets.

"No to the hitting, Neil, but I'll be honest," I said, trying to catch Neil's eye. I am that kind of guy, honest to the core, but Neil didn't appear interested, so I poured a few more Junior Mints into his hand, hoping to get his attention because this was important. I didn't want Neil on my bad side. He's the future. Exactly like my kids, who need me, and I need them and Robin. "Neil!" I cried, tears rolling over my lips, ruining the chocolate mint flavor I love with a hint of salt from my tears. I know some love the combination of salt and chocolate, but I hate it.

"NEIL," I shouted. "I didn't hit anyone!" Neil ran out of the room, and I followed him, chasing his bare bottom. "Neil, listen. Robin and I were fighting over some photographs, and you know they're mine. I took them! Well, you may not know, but when you were a baby, I took your picture, or maybe not yours, but I took other kids' photos. Photography is my thing--on the side, of course. And I love rock and roll, Neil. Good rock and roll, and I would've played what Robin liked if she just asked. I resent music coming under the heading of how selfish I am. You can't taint music--I won't let her."

Neil crawled backward down the stairs, which at his age seemed babyish. He didn't look at me, but I kept telling him everything. Thank god he listened or at least didn't talk because, in the long run, you want to spill your guts to someone who takes it all in. Why hide the truth, I realized, especially when you're in the right? And then it dawned on me that these people--the Richardsons--are practically family and have been waiting for me to realize this simple fact. They probably have been waiting for me to turn up--even if they didn't know it.

"To continue, Neil: we had our hands on a photo of the kids I took in the backyard. A totally beautiful black and white shot. Robin pulled so hard on the frame that I lost my balance. Then, I'll admit it. I lost my head and hip checked her. She landed on the wall, hardly made a noise, and we tussled. The minute I gave up, she hugged the photo to her chest and went berserk. Before I knew it, she'd called the cops. They wrote it up as domestic violence, which is crap, Neil. Pure crap." Richard appeared downstairs looking much worse for the wear. He said he had to go to the hardware store to get new pliers.

"These just broke apart," he said, holding high two halves of an old pair of pliers. "Neil, get your pants on, honey, and on the way home we'll go by the cemetery where Mommy is dancing. You'll like that."

"Boy, I'd love to photograph Sally in a cemetery! How random and cool," I said, slipping on an old newspaper they'd obviously used to sop up water or maybe some ice they dragged in on their boots. "Maybe I'll wait here," I said. "We could all do dinner later? Make it together like the old days when Robin and I would invite friends over. Before we moved, of course, and I'm embarrassed and really sorry that we never invited you. I don't know why we never had you and Sally over. I mean, you are practically family. Did I tell you the mayor came to our anniversary party?" Richard filled the dog's water bowl and sloshed some on the floor, soaking the newspaper under the kitty litter. "Of all our friends, you're the first people I thought of when this situation blew up. Let me make it up to you, forgetting to have you over and everything. You guys go, you and Neil, and I'll whip up something as a surprise for Sally."

Then, out of nowhere, Neil asked the dog--this poor old mangy dog--to bite me.

"Get him," Neil said, pointing at me. "Get him," he yelled over and over until finally Richard, who'd been fooling with his keys, trying, I guess, to get a key off his key ring or maybe get one on the ring, asked Neil again to get his pants on. Neil ran off with the dog following.

I think the reindeer debacle exhausted Richard because he literally collapsed on a kitchen stool, the keys now dangling at his side. I asked him what his impressions of Robin had been, whether he'd seen this coming or not. He admitted that he hadn't seen it coming but then reminded me that we hadn't seen each other that much over the years. That, I told him, was Robin's fault. Of course, I didn't say that she really disliked him and Sally (I think I have already gotten that across), but just that she didn't like socializing, which wasn't really true. Richard nodded but then squinted hard.

"Where the heck is Neil?" he asked, standing up slowly, looking around like maybe Neil would materialize out of thin air if he looked long enough.

"Upstairs," I said. "Remember--the pants?"

"Yeah, but he should be here by now, I think." I followed Richard upstairs.

"So how do you like the dinner idea?" I asked, staying close at Richard's heels. "I make a mean burger!"

"Um, well, I would have to check with Sally, and anyway, she's a vegetarian along with Neil. Hey, what's going on?" Richard suddenly yelled. "Neil!" he yelled, running to the office with me close behind. "Oh my god, oh my god," he shouted with his head out the window. "I forgot to shut the window!"

I saw Neil, still half-naked on the roof with both arms around the reindeer and the stupid dog slipping toward the gutter on the icy tar roof.

"Neil!" Richard reached both arms out the window. Why he didn't just go out on the roof, I wasn't sure, unless throwing a line out is a better method for saving someone than going straight to the victim, in this case a kid, and inadvertently pushing him to his death. Neil must've been freezing.

"I will only come back in if he leaves," Neil yelled, crawling slowly toward the window. "My knees are frozen," he screamed.

"C'mon, Neil," Richard coaxed.

"Only if that crying man leaves," he yelled so loud I thought the neighbors heard about all my sobbing.

"But what about dinner?" I yelled. I really hoped to eat with these guys.

"Michael, I think, well, you might have to take off," Richard said, still reaching to Neil.

"My knees are frozen and so are my feet," Neil yelled again.

"C'mon, Neil," I yelled as loud as I could. "I'll warm your knees." Then the kid just went nuts and I found myself flying down the stairs and out the door, which Richard had never succeeded in shutting. I was in my car halfway to nowhere when I realized I'd left my coat in the kitchen. I did a U-turn, practically getting broadsided by a guy who gave me the finger. I was about to give it right back to him, when I saw Katherine Montauk and her husband Ray chopping at a bedraggled looking forsythia bush. I pulled to the curb and rolled down my window.

"Hey, friends." I smiled. They stood, flushed, and Ray was clutching his back. Katherine pulled her hat off and shook her head like she was dizzy from getting upright so fast. "Good to see you," I said, getting out of the car. We stared at each other for an uncomfortable amount of time until I introduced myself and they both nodded.

HOTLINE

Oh, wow. Miracles do happen. I guess I should say, "thanks for picking up." I mean, I've only been waiting for, like, an hour. Look, I'm calling because I'm wondering about something. It's sort of convoluted, but I figure you'll understand being a hotline and all.

So it started last summer with an outdoor performance--I have a small dance company, and one of my dancers sort of took up residence in my house while we rehearsed. Actually, every one of my dancers moved into my basement, which was really stressful. They were all sort of homeless at the same time, and to make matters worse, the dancer who stayed the longest was really sick. He had diarrhea, like, twenty-four hours a day--in my house. But he didn't tell me he had AIDS; he just said he had a pesticide--I mean a parasite--that he got in Russia. I guess that's not a weird thing to get in Russia, which makes you wonder, shouldn't the water supply be, like, the country's main preoccupation, other than the Bolshoi, of course. Well, one thing is for sure: take Russia off your list of edifying vacations.

Anyway, here's the background, which, don't worry, is totally, like, not attenuated, meaning, you know, long. When my three-year-old son sits on the toilet, he puts his hands on either side of the seat for balance. Right off the bat, the parasite went from his hands to his mouth, which I know is beyond eew. Then he got sick, but my seven-year-old daughter got really sick. At first, it was like a mystery you were too afraid to solve. She lost weight and slept--we could barely get her out of bed. The doctor couldn't fathom that she had a parasite, since, duh, we live in the United States, so for a couple of months she wasted away. She had little to lose in the first place. She only weighed eleven pounds on her first birthday. We're naturally thin people, although some of us take it to extremes. My cousin is six feet four and weighs about one forty. He's anorexic and refuses to admit it. I was, too, but for dancers it's like a mandatory affliction--a rite of passage if it doesn't kill you. You know, air-popped popcorn and hard-boiled eggs minus the yolk. But he's a nuclear physicist so being skeletal is hardly a requirement.

Anyway, I was a wreck. I teach dance and I could barely do a plie without sitting down. I worried about my daughter nonstop but couldn't do much because I was totally exhausted. Let me tell you, I have new respect for people in the third world. You know how people say they should just work harder? Well, you try getting one of these parasites--it's mind-boggling how tired you are. I mean, balancing a basket on my head would've been impossible, let alone digging up tubers or I guess working the night shift in some claustrophobic factory.

Well, finally the doctor said, 'Take your poop to a clinic,'--which is impossible for kids. You try telling them to go just a little. It all comes out. I had cottage cheese containers full of poop. I couldn't get the top on.

It seemed like forever before the lab figured it out--but really it was only a few days later when I got a call while I was teaching Intermediate Modern. Usually, I don't pick up while I'm in the middle of teaching, but this time I turned down the music and whispered, 'Hello.' Someone said, 'You've got Giardia.' My students were dumbfounded when I began to jump up and down, screaming, 'Yes, yes, yes.' I mean, how many people are ecstatic to find out they have a parasite? But at least I knew what we had. I thought we were dying a mysterious death like in the Middle Ages, which I guess wasn't a mystery since they thought God was punishing them for being terrible people. This may sound weird, but whipping away guilt sounds really comforting at this point. Dancing the Tarantella sounds even better.

I mean, why guilt and why all the time? Well, not all the time because after I hung up with whoever called me, my thoughts vanished and my brain emptied itself like I was back in ballet class letting the savior of dance seep into me. Something about music and movement linked together like a chain link fence banishes every little bit of guilt. The thoughts that remind you of your inherent evilness, the ones that spring up like weeds, just go limp once you place your feet in a perfectly straight line, toes to either side, even if you force your turnout, which every self-respecting teacher tells you not to do, but you know she doesn't mean it. Results are everything in ballet, which I find comforting, and probably anyone who sticks with it feels the same. In between two extremes is kind of nothing, let's face it.

Anyway, after I said goodbye to whoever gave me the good news, I became energized, and I made a great combination of mainly jumps and turns, which shows how much is in your mind and, I guess, in your body. No guilt in a *plie* and definitely not in a jump. Dance is a godsend to the guilt-ridden and, let's face it, the mentally-ill, and once you've got the dance disease in your veins you realize that people who don't dance are just empty, boring people walking around like slobs. Oh, sorry. Don't feel bad; it's not your fault you don't dance, or maybe it is. I have no idea. You probably just have good mental health for no apparent reason other than you got lucky.

So back to the point. Yesterday, I started feeling really guilty about Mark--yeah, the dancer with AIDS, because I didn't go to his funeral. Well, I was really mad at his family. They'd never seen him dance or supported him or anything, and I didn't want to meet them at his funeral. But actually, I didn't care an iota about his family. I didn't go because I have this travel fear and the funeral was in Hartford, and I don't know if you've ever been to Hartford but it's a very confusing town; it sort of goes round and round. I actually haven't been there, but that's how I imagine it from what people have said. If I'm gonna get up the guts to leave Providence, go somewhere, it's New York. The whole place is a grid: boom, boom, boom. At this point, I have trouble getting to my teaching job, which is, like, a half hour away, but I'm hoping one day to get back to New York, a place I love because everyone seems preoccupied and, I'm hoping, guilt-ridden. I'm not sure if it's guilt, but, right out of the bus you confront a sea of worried faces, which makes me want to shout hallelujah. I'm not the only one; I'm not the only one.

Anyway, so then this guilt over not conquering my travel fears (that's what my dad always told me to do, and he should know since he could barely get out the backdoor) so that I could do important things like go to Mark's funeral exploded into a bigger worry that I might be responsible for killing my entire family.

Okay, here's my question: can you get AIDS by getting Giardia from a person who has Giardia who has AIDS?

YOU DON'T KNOW? What do you mean, you don't know? I mean, this is the National Aids Hotline. I thought you've probably answered this question alone over five million times today? No one's ever asked you this question? I imagined you the whole time I had to wait through "Sitting on the Dock of the Bay" over and over again saying 'no, you can't get it that way,' and we'd be done with it. Bingo--I'd be on to a new guilty worry after, you know, a moment or two of relief.

You have to call who? A consulting doctor? Can you call me right back? I know it's five o'clock on a Friday, but I can't live with this. Could I stay on the line? No? Look, if you can't get him, call me back anyway, there's more we can talk about. I can't believe I didn't go to Mark's funeral. I mean, it was never an option, really. And actually, I couldn't care less. My dad didn't go to his own brother's funeral, and not just because of the travel fear, but that's a situation you don't want to hear about, although it's kind of interesting since it involves disinheritance. But unless some miracle happens and I stop feeling guilty twenty-four-seven, I'll take the guilt of not going to a funeral over the death of my whole family. I hope this doesn't ruin your life, but I'm really depending on you. But don't lie or sugarcoat the truth. I can take it. Thoughts are gonna kill me anyway. Dad said they aren't real. But I know they are.

LIFE SUPPORT

"Corny, you gotta phone call. Seems that Bay's going to hospice tonight." As Dale, the skeletal home aide, slipped into a jacket meant for someone a size or two bigger, he motioned Dad to the phone. Dad waved him away and I took a deep breath. I had just arrived in Muncie after a budget flight involving no less than three stops. I'd hoped this Dale could stay for a while, help me get my bearings and deal with Dad.

"Hey, that's too bad, but my dinner's getting cold," Dad said, hovering over his plate of chicken tenders.

"He's kind of busy now," Dale said into the phone and then flew out the front door, his jacket flapping like a parachute.

Years ago, a few days after we cremated my mother, Dad found Bay alone in a booth at the IHOP. She wasn't the first woman he'd considered for the job of post-Mom life support. As an agoraphobic, he had been quick to start building up a list of potential candidates--sort of like Mitt Romney's binders of women. Fill-ins from any walk of life and looks didn't matter. I had watched him snuggle up to a homely radiologist as she traced the outlines of Mom's ovarian cancer on the X-ray he ignored.

"Fourth stage," she announced, and before I finished wiping my eyes, Dad asked her on a date.

"There's a picture at the Lucon--my treat."

"Show Mr. Wood to the bereavement lounge," she'd whispered to the nurse.

On the afternoon we picked up Mom's ashes, he spotted a woman at the bus stop outside the crematorium.

"Call me Irma," she whispered, sliding into the back seat of Dad's white Cadillac. When she offered Dad a red licorice whip and pointed to a motel, I opted to walk home, ferrying Mom's ashes in my backpack. Mom had little interest in ritual, but she might object to being stored in Dad's backseat as he drove around town looking for her replacement.

"She's from Ukraine and keeps a stash of rubber gloves in her purse. You can't imagine what a prostate exam feels like!"

"You're right," I said, as he described getting his first one in the motel's kitchen where Irma worked the breakfast shift.

When Irma proved normal, or at least not mentally ill like Mom and Bay, she hit Dad, screaming that if he wouldn't take her to Florida he could get lost.

"Boy, I'll miss those exams and her see-through blouses."

I guess Dad liked Bay for the mystery, or at least he didn't mind that she would not let him know where she lived. While they strolled the aisles of K-Mart--their meeting spot of choice--Bay admitted that her real name was Anna but some people called her Marilyn. Having been a reporter, Dad had lots of experience smoking out a story, and he loved reading people's minds. When I picked him up at K-Mart's garden shop, he was beginning to think that she might have a criminal past.

"On the other hand," he mused, "she might be a nun." A few weeks after the funeral and internment of Mom's ashes, I drove east to graduate school, not realizing that I would not see my father for ten years. For a while, I tried to hold onto him, but he rarely answered his phone or returned messages. If he answered the phone, he would beg to get off. Bay--always around--needed him. *At least he's not describing a blow job*, I thought.

Busy, married with a new job, I decided it was the typical disintegration of a family after the mother's death--even a bipolar mother. But after a friend from high school discovered Dad and Bay's marriage notice in an old *Indy Star*, my sense of injustice kicked in.

"How could you not invite me?" I asked Bay. "Could I talk to Dad?"

"He detests you and your dead mother." My hatred for them was sealed.

"My mother was a brilliant artist who looked like Ingrid Bergman, for your information," I yelled before hanging up. Then I sobbed, remembering my adolescent intolerance for my mother's bi-polar mood swings.

One year, Bay, in an enraged voicemail, accused us of trying to get Dad's money. I vowed to stop all communication. As usual, I lost my resolve, calling within a month. Bay said if I called again, they'd move to Panama after having me jailed.

The dream of adventure was pure Dad, but the violence and finality was outside his realm. How many times had he told me to keep life fluid and steer clear of the government? Besides, I never asked Dad for a penny. Night after night, I tossed in bed, swatting my pillow, punching it like Dad was inside and I could knock sense into his brain. Could Bay be like the cruel sister in *What Ever Happened to Baby Jane*? I'd finally fall asleep, reminding myself that he was strong like a bull and could protect himself--against what, I wasn't sure.

After I had a second kid, I barely communicated with him until Cheryl from Adult Protective Services called. When you're old, I discovered, the state checks up on you. They even do your grocery shopping and make your meals. They don't usually call the police unless someone throws a mug of vodka at them or they find a naked person in a wheelchair playing with a roaring fire.

"I told your dad I wouldn't budge until he gave me someone's number," Cheryl said. "He'd told me you were dead. Then I saw a letter with your return address." I welled up. "He's building fires from his wheelchair and not fully dressed." After some throat clearing, she whispered that he usually answers the door naked.

"That's nothing new," I said, remembering him parading around the house, his flesh red from drying in front of a blazing fire.

"We got the first call after Bay threw a mug of vodka at a caseworker," Cheryl said.

"Vodka?"

"We found about fifty gallon bottles under a bush in the front yard. I guess she throws her mug at your dad, otherwise how'd he get all the bumps on his head?"

I listened to Cheryl relate Dad's lies about my untimely death at the hands of a serial murderer and descriptions of Bay's drunken rages while I booked a flight to Muncie on my laptop.

"I guess we'll see you soon, but I can't tell you how glad I am to find you now that her foot fell off and the other's about to follow suit."

"Her foot did what?"

"We didn't see that her feet and hands were black because she always wore mittens and slippers. Said she had to protect herself from the sun," Cheryl paused. "I found the foot, and that's not easy to forget."

The flight was a blur. It wasn't until I was about to ring the bell that I began to tremble. Would Bay be back from the hospital with no feet? I knocked and rang the bell.

"I bet it's your daughter!" I recognized Dale's voice, hiring him had been mandated by Adult Protective Services. He flung open the door and was about to encircle me in a hug when the phone rang. He ran off as Dad yelled for help with the ketchup. I dropped my suitcase in the hall and ran to the kitchen.

"Hey, can you get the top off the ketchup?" Dad asked before gulping a McDonald's shake. I remembered he hated straws and that greetings were a waste of time, but I'd been away too long to immediately revert to our old ways. My stomach tightened, and I slumped into a chair. "After dinner, let's go to the IHOP for a sundae." He wiped his milk mustache with the back of his hand.

"Okay--should we check on Bay first?"

"Maybe tomorrow. You never know who we'll meet at the IHOP, and they close at nine."

CUT TO THE CHASE

Seven bridesmaids sporting identical gray zip-up hoodies filed into the dressing room of The Pompeo Club. Their diaphanous gowns, no two alike in style and color, hung to the floor.

"Don't call them 'pink,'" one of the bridesmaids had scolded the photographer earlier that morning. "We're subverting gender identification as it pertains to color--or something like that."

Likewise, unruly hairstyles disrupted the space. "I feel like I have twigs coming out of my head," the only teenager in the group whispered.

"It's a denial of the corps mentality," said Diane, a former ballet dancer who'd written a dissertation on the politics of alternative beauty performance.

"Or just not smooth and, you know, typical," the stylist said as she lined up the bridesmaids for another spray.

"I'd call it," Diane said tossing the little braids she'd requested from the accommodating stylist, "a fuck you to the misogyny of the department store, the cookie cutter, the stranglehold of capitalism and conformity.

"Hi, guys! You all look so beautiful." Helen, the bride, her long blonde hair half up in a ramshackle bun, emerged from behind a screen and smiled at the seven young women. "Can you guys start on the cake?"

Cassandra, a bridesmaid Helen had known since nursery school, took a breath, her brown eyes widening as she stared at the towering fake cake Helen had ordered from an artist specializing in cardboard creations. Still bruised from losing the battle with Helen over hairstyles and dresses--she preferred the constructivist designs of Oskar Schlemmer to Helen's predilection for post-modern randomness--Cassandra's stomach churned imagining a haphazard decorating scheme, a fake cake toppling under the weight of too much disparity.

"The flowers are in the box. A few broke, but she made extras." Helen searched her stuff for the photo of the cake she'd picked from the artist's website. "The picture's here--somewhere!"

Cassandra backed up, slipped off her hoodie, and stretched her tattooed arms to either side, forcing the bridesmaids into a huddle at her back.

"It's our job to keep the bride calm," she whispered. "Believe me, I know." The stylist nodded, hoping Cassandra would describe a personal tragedy. Instead, Cassandra stared ahead, avoiding distractions.

"Found it!" Helen waved a photo of the five–tier fake cake decorated in a spiraling floral pattern with little birds hovering over each layer.

"Beautiful." Sally, the pregnant bridesmaid, smiled at Helen. A cousin once removed, Sally had worried that peripatetic Helen might never get married. When Helen called with news of her engagement and a giddy request for Sally to be maid of honor, she consented even though the wedding fell dangerously close to her due date.

"Oh, yes." She had not hesitated, figuring she might be responsible for saving the wedding if Helen's parents derailed the day. No one in the family could forget the Thanksgiving when Helen's father, Philip, left the turkey in the trunk of his car and then couldn't find the keys. Worse was another holiday when Helen's mother, Annette, a performance artist, threw a plate of spaghetti at her sister because she had nearly ruined Annette's site-specific performance at a hazardous waste site by forgetting to wear the protective suit. Now, trying not to stare at Cassandra's many tattoos of Greek deities, Sally worried about Helen's friends as well.

"Beautiful," Sally said again.

Cassandra turned her back to Helen and gave Sally a stern look. Then she left the group, advancing toward Helen in bold strides.

"Not possible! You are going to have to wrap your head around the fact that we can't accomplish *that*," she stabbed at the photo. Then she shook her head, flinging her red bobbed hair about her cheeks, a signal, perhaps, for something unattainable.

"Let's try," Helen raised her eyebrows, picturing a late-night request for forgiveness. Just last month Cassandra had excoriated Helen in a text for wearing the wrong shoes on a double date. When Helen didn't respond, Cassandra called, ruining a deep sleep.

"I'm very sorry, but I've warned you about the deleterious effect heels have on crowds. Some compare them to car alarms and sirens. Besides, I wanted you to wear flats so we'd match. Guys love stuff like that." Helen reminded her that the call began as an apology.

Cassandra snatched the photo from Helen, scrunched it into a ball, and tossed it into someone's coffee. Quick as a flash, Sally searched the photo on her phone and secreted it in the pouch of her hoodie to the bridesmaid who, over a breakfast of ancient grains, confessed to the bridal party that she'd changed her name from Amanda to Aerial now that she'd taken up acro yoga fulltime. With their backs to Cassandra, Sally and Aerial began to insert the fake flowers and birds into the nearly invisible holes scattered all over the cardboard cake iced in glistening fake icing.

Cassandra was about to announce the countdown to a mandatory once-over for fuzzies and lipstick smudges, when a groomsman, disregarding the GIRLS ONLY sign, barged into the dressing room, banging the swinging door into a mirror that luckily withstood the crash.

"Out," Cassandra said, yanking from his hands a box containing the real cake Helen's wedding planner ordered from Costco. She squinted at the label, her eyes widening slowly like an inflating balloon.

Before scurrying away with the cake, Cassandra looked around for witnesses. Helen stared in the mirror the stylist held. Others hovered around the fake cake decorators and their slowly transforming creation. Emma, Helen's teenage niece, suggested posting the original photo alongside a photo of the finished fake cake.

"We shouldn't gloat," Sally whispered, looking around for Cassandra.

"Why not?" Emma asked, tapping the Instagram icon.

"Disaster! I knew it." Cassandra had locked herself in a bathroom before texting the real cake bearing groomsman. "May Day, May Day," she wrote and then, in desperation, phoned him. "Finally," she said after he cleared his throat like he had to prepare to speak into a phone. "I'll cut to the chase," she said, glaring at a soap dispenser--a modern convenience full of chemicals she once tore off a wall, taping over the holes the ingredients for real soap and signing Joseph Bueys at the bottom. "We have an impending disaster on our hands. This is a cream cheese cake that won't be consumed for approximately two to ten hours, at which time it will be poison, riddled with salmonella due to a lack of refrigeration. Find a car; we'll take it back to the Costco that deserves to be firebombed for nearly killing everyone at this wedding." After reapplying her lipstick, she shrouded the cake with her hoodie and hurried outside.

The groomsman, made aware of the lethal nature of an unrefrigerated cream cheese cake, ran a stop sign and drove over a bump-out to return to the place he'd just left in a car he borrowed from a groomsman so hungover from the post-rehearsal dinner bar crawl he wouldn't remember loaning the car. Hiding behind a tree, Cassandra popped from the shadows the minute she spied the groomsman. She slid the cake into the backseat and quietly closed the door, still afraid of being discovered by anyone in the wedding party. No one understood food poisoning as she did, having once worked on an archaeological dig that unearthed the stunted bones of ancient Greeks cut down in their prime due to the consumption of moldy, unrefrigerated food.

"Go!" she commanded in a stage whisper as she adjusted the outside mirror.

"Okay, okay," he said, readjusting the mirror as he pumped the gas pedal. "Oh right, the leaky gas tank. Wouldn't ya know it's almost empty."

"I knew you weren't the right person," Cassandra hissed, once again shaking her red hair but this time slower like she, too, was close to empty.

That's when Helen's father pulled up and all four of his windows went down.

"You two can either save this wedding or not," Cassandra announced as if Helen's father knew all about the fatal cake.

"The Costco is a ways away." The groomsman stared at his GPS.

"I assume you have gas," Cassandra said to Helen's father.

"The wedding's in two hours," he said, checking the sun as he talked to himself, a habit his wife found annoying.

"Exactly." Cassandra signaled the groomsman to get the cake out of the nearly gasless car. He saluted, got the cake, and wedged himself into the Mini Helen's parents rented.

"What are we up to?" Helen's father asked the groomsman as they drove to Costco.

After losing each other in the aisles of the cavernous store, Helen's father found the groomsman at the returns desk.

"I texted you," the groomsman said, pushing the cart behind a woman returning a large cactus. Helen's father frowned like he was tired of hearing about this *texting*.

"So, this isn't a cream cheese cake," the clerk at the returns desk said, pointing to the white label.

"Ow!" Helen's father whacked the returned cactus as he searched his head for the reading glasses he'd forgotten.

"Oh, right." The groomsman nodded at the clerk like he'd known all along about the cake's mistaken identity.

"The order was for deluxe cream icing and that's what you got."

Together, the men picked up the cake, placing it carefully into the carriage like pallbearers lowering a coffin. Then they rushed outside, swerving around cars until they saw a woman in a Costco uniform, copying a license.

"Some dope left the lights on," she said, lighting a cigarette.

"But that's not his car--it's a rental," the groomsman said.

"That's a first," she laughed.

"It takes fifteen hours, on average, for a battery to die," Helen's father said as he popped the trunk.

"I wouldn't put a cake in the trunk," the Costco worker said as Helen's father peered inside.

"There's my suit, but where's the shoe bag?" The woman leaned forward, checking Philip's ring finger.

"We don't sell dress shoes if that's what you're missing," she said, blowing smoke into the trunk.

"Did you forget them?" the groomsman asked, unaware that Philip, a social historian with a field in statistics, hated questions unaccompanied by data.

The groomsman sucked in his cheeks. The father of the bride with no shoes could make you laugh, and this was no laughing matter, the groomsman recognized, as Helen's father, swearing in a voice that got louder and louder, rummaged in the near-empty trunk.

"I've got a pair of black boots you could wear, sort of shiny with lots of metal studs," he said, comparing Philip's smaller foot with his own. "Hey, I'll call a tux rental store--size nine?" The groomsman waved his phone at Helen's father who nodded and frowned.

"I did not leave the bag on the plane," he said, picturing Annette with raised eyebrows.

"Good luck, gentlemen, and get that car started before you have more on your hands than a pair of missing shoes."

"Do you have black dress shoes?" the groomsman said into his phone as the two men screeched through the Costco parking lot--an ocean of asphalt that seemed to have no exits but lots of curbs guiding one back to Costco. "Got 'em!" the groomsman said, hoping Helen's father, who narrowly missed a shopping cart, might think of him as a son or at least a competent accomplice. "They're waiting for us!"

After more swearing, they escaped Costco by running over a curb next to a ramp, which on this day was clogged with Saturday traffic.

"I'm supposed to be working on my toast," Helen's father realized when they finally arrived at Tuxedo Junction. The groomsman was back in no time with the shoes, and after more hair-raising driving on Philip's part, he delivered the cake to Sally through a side door of The Pompeo Club.

"Tell Cassandra it's safe," the groomsman whispered.

"She's lying down with a migraine," Sally said, raising her newly threaded eyebrows. The groomsman raised his eyebrows before running back to the Mini to find Philip wincing as he tried to remember the other parents' names. Annette had told him a million times to welcome them warmly since they'd agreed to pay half the wedding costs.

"I'm changing in your room," Philip announced as he pulled into the Seaside Hotel parking lot. "I don't have time to drive to my hotel." He didn't want to admit that he couldn't remember how to get there. It suddenly didn't seem fair that his wife was allowed to change next door at the Pompeo Club.

"Lot's full; we'll have to try the spillover lot across the highway," the groomsman said, clicking out of a dating site. Helen's father pulled a U-turn as he practiced his opening remarks about the joys of unexpected news he thought led perfectly into a story about Helen, at ten, announcing over the phone that she'd successfully put out a kitchen fire.

"You shouldn't melt butter in the toaster oven," he said, pretending to be Helen as he drifted into the highway.

"Turn into the lot!" the groomsman yelled as a truck honked and swerved. Helen's father jerked the car into a tight spot and the men took off--the groomsman clutching the bag of shoes.

"You forgot your suit!"

"Right, right." Helen's father raced back to the car, where he pressed his body against the trunk to avoid a car racing to grab the last parking spot. Without thinking, he clicked open the trunk. It flew up, hitting him in the chin before he could jump back.

"Jesus Christ," he yelled, clutching his chin as he grabbed the suit. With both hands occupied, he forgot to close the trunk and instead left it wide open as he rushed to catch up with the groomsman.

The men straddled a Jersey barrier, Helen's father holding his chin in one hand and the suit high up in the other. A truck barreled past, whipping the groomsman's comb over to one side of his head where it hung like a ripped curtain. Car after car zoomed past until, in a traffic break, the men raced across the four lanes.

In the room, Helen's father stripped down to his boxers, black socks, and T-shirt. On went the starched shirt, the blue tie, and the black suit jacket. The groomsman put on his pants and smiled.

"Almost ready!" Helen's father breathed a sigh of relief as he reached for an empty hanger, the hanger with no pants.

"Maybe your wife has them?" The groomsman shrugged like he was out of solutions. As much as Philip wanted to call Annette, he was tortured by her performance of another humiliating episode involving the splitting of his pants seam minutes before he was to deliver a paper. In a downtown New York loft, she'd slowly ripped the seam of her own pants standing in an overhead special. Luckily, there were only about eight people in the audience, and during the Q and A following the performance, she mercifully refused to divulge the performance's source.

Resisting the urge to call her, he fled the room and the groomsman, then on his hands and knees searching for a cufflink.

"Who cares about a cufflink?" Helen's father thought as he ran into the lobby and begged the clerk for news of the missing pants.

"You lost your pants?" The clerk peered over the desk at Helen's father's bare legs and black socks.

Outside, squinting into the sun, he spotted a black heap in the far lane of the highway. A puddle of oil, he thought. Besides, pants dropped on a highway would be ruined, ripped, covered in tire marks. He checked the sun and then his watch. He'd been warned to be in line at the Pompeo Club in fifteen minutes. He needed to ignore this mirage and find his dry-cleaned, unharmed pants. Or some pants.

It occurred to him as sweat rolled down his temples that finding the pants was statistically dismal.

"You know you have no pants on, right?" The clerk ducked his head out the electric door.

"Can I borrow yours?" The clerk, eyes bugging, pointed to a woman in a long pinkish dress on the far side of the highway holding a pair of pants, the pants that were not a puddle of oil, not a mirage. The groomsman, spiffy in his black suit, emerged from the hotel with Philip's rental shoes.

"Hey, that's Cassandra holding the pants! I wonder if she has a boyfriend?" The groomsman waved as Cassandra ran across the highway clutching the pants.

"It's a good thing I noticed your trunk was open or I'd never have found these!" Cassandra thrust the pants at Philip.

"We might keep this to ourselves," he said, slipping on the pants as a family, staring ahead, emerged through the revolving door into the glaring sunlight. "Annette doesn't need to know," he added, imagining Annette on stage in her underpants and a pair of his black socks, begging a stranger for his pants.

"We solved the cake problem!" The groomsman offered Cassandra his arm.

"I knew you'd take care of it," she said as they set off for the Pompeo Club on foot. Philip trailed, finishing the toast with the story of Helen dropping her passport in a sewer. *A perfect ending*, he thought, *especially the part about someone finding the passport days later floating in the Thames.*

THE PRESSING FOUNDATION

The pressing in my stomach began a while back--not sure when. My brain refuses to organize time. If I look back, I see a scramble of events. Like, who can say when my neighbor with the face of a wolfhound fell in love with me? That episode when we rode around my hometown of East Lansing in his Chevy Bel Air with the powder blue interior and the seatbelts draped over the seats--we didn't know you were supposed to wear them--is mixed up with my falling in love with a boy whose sister was crowned Miss Michigan. The two memories pop up at the same time because the neighbor's wife had been Miss Iowa; at least that's what I heard.

Anyway, back to the pressing in my stomach. Dr. Laude's nurse asked how long I'd had the pressing. Feels like forever, although certainly not since the day my husband and I moved to Rhode Island thirty years ago. Not since our kids left for college and never returned. But as the nurse breathed into the phone, I couldn't remember what it was like not to have the pressing.

"One month?"

"How's tomorrow at ten?"

That night, at the Preserve Providence Fundraiser, I drained a glass of Prosecco and the pressing stopped. The waiter nodded like he'd been sent to stop the pressing. By the next morning, I realized that, along with Prosecco, sleep stopped the pressing, which gave me hope. No way cancer would take a break from winding its way through the body each night. Wouldn't sleep be the cure for cancer?

When Dr. Laude pulled back the curtain, I informed her that the pressing in my stomach indicated cancer. She said she wouldn't go there right off the bat.

After some stomach kneading, she pronounced the pressing a result of anxiety. I almost hugged her. My nerves finally helped me out. Even though I knew the pressing was real, at least now I had it on good authority that it wasn't.

The next morning, I called the nurse in a daze.

"I can't sit up." She put me on hold for, like, an hour, cutting off the second verse of "Stayin' Alive" to let me know that Dr. Laude consented to a sonogram. Dr. Laude thinks tests are a waste of time, which is why I chose her as my doctor. Nothing is worse in my mind than windowless rooms with steel doors.

After I explained to the receptionist at the imaging center that I needed to first see the inside of the sonogram room, she FaceTimed the room even though FaceTiming is against protocol. (Her niece has a lot of problems, so she's used to doing weird things. Like, once she had to hide the Comet in her underwear drawer so her niece wouldn't worry about poisoning everyone at her birthday party). Fear of windowless rooms is nothing, she said.

During the sonogram, I told the technician she probably knew more than the radiologist, hoping she'd divulge what she saw as she rubbed the instrument around my stomach. She frowned and rubbed harder.

After she wiped the gel off my stomach, I raced to my dance studio for the last rehearsal before the recital. Just as I got the front line in first arabesque, Dr. Laude called. She never calls unless she must tell me something, like I don't need a test for diabetes because I don't have any of the symptoms.

"They found mixed cysts--you have a CAT scan tomorrow." I breathed out. At least now I could forget about dying and worry about the CAT scan and how not to have it.

"Could I go straight to surgery?"

She ignored my question. If only we could keep talking, I thought, I might get her laughing. But then I remembered that I'd never been able to get her laughing. Once I said she could fire me. Instead of laughing, she said that would be unethical.

"Remember, no eating after midnight tonight."

"I'll never eat again," I said, hoping a bout of anorexia might change this condition into something I could just talk about with a therapist. We hung up, and it felt like letting go of a balloon. No Dr. Laude anymore, and when I see my husband, I'll realize that I won't see him for much longer. That's why I let the students go early. I didn't want to see anyone I wouldn't see again.

Then I thought of my neighbor, a doctor who believes in herbs, not medicine. Perhaps he would know how to cure cysts with honey. I rushed to his house.

He wrinkled his forehead when I asked about mixed cysts and hurried away, returning with a big book entitled *Civilization and Man.*

"I need to ask your husband about the Crusades." People always ask my husband about world history or the civil war, even after he explains that he's a historian of the Progressive Era and hasn't thought much about an alternate theory of who killed Lincoln.

I hurried home, wondering where the heck he was. I'd called him a bunch of times and was miffed to be robbed of a dramatic announcement. I wanted to sob and hear him say his life would be nothing without me. Instead, per usual, he either didn't hear his phone or left it at the library. I called again, realizing that not only did he get to live he also got to be at the center of my funeral where everyone would console him, a performance opportunity I guiltily admitted I'd imagined for myself. What good was marrying someone ten years older to be outlived?

Then he arrived in an absent-minded stupor.

"I called you a million times." I dished guilt until I got bored with his protests about the difficulty of the iPhone and how much he missed his flip phone. After he sank into his chair, I told him the news.

"Cysts?"

"Mixed cysts!" I said, like he'd confused an exotic medley of olives for the plain variety.

Then, like any good historian, he spent the evening researching cysts.

"Probably a GIST," he announced, like he'd morphed from a Ph.D, to an M.D. His lovely symmetrical face wavered before my eyes. How long would it be until someone else owned that face? I imagined the kids holding his hands.

"We won't hate you, Dad, if you date." Those traitors, I wailed silently.

"They're curable," he said, closing his laptop like we could now forget about them. I nodded, dwelling on the aftermath of my funeral. He was absent-minded for sure but always had a practical side.

"I'd like to order something for my girlfriend," he'd say on the first Valentine's Day after my death. Wait until she finds his gross Kleenexes on her side of the bed, his constant nose blowing (he has sinusitis, which is a term for a constantly running nose), and his devotion to beer, which he'd admitted (although he denies it) was number one in his life, me and the kids coming in second.

Then again, meeting people wasn't his forte. A handsome, brainy guy, wonderfully sarcastic with a naturally subversive bent couldn't connect. I met him by knocking on his door, borrowing things like sugar until finally, he asked me out.

The next morning, the CAT scan technician laid me down on a wide bed, placing my arms in an archaic modern dance shape before hurrying to a control panel outside the room I was now trapped in. She couldn't risk exposure to radiation day in and day out, but on the other hand, shouldn't she stay with her patients, sacrificing herself as part of the job?

Then a voice directed me to hold my breath as a bar flew overhead. I followed the directions with the precision you might expect from a ballet teacher. But really, my perfect breathing was just a bargain: if I follow directions I'll be guaranteed a positive outcome.

"All done," the woman said, pointing to the door. I'd survived basically nothing and yet pride flooded over me. I'd performed an adult role and that had to be the most anyone could ask of me--God, the devil, or even Dr. Laude.

"I'll park the car." My husband ferried me to Dr. Laude's door in a downpour. As I extended one leg into the pouring rain, I imagined him confiding in a colleague that even the weather foreshadowed my demise. The minute I opened the door to the waiting room, I knew I was doomed. It was lunchtime, the place was empty, and the lone receptionist who maybe didn't deserve lunch whispered into the phone. Then I heard Dr. Laude's voice.

"Okay, I see," she said. She hung up and swung around as I backed away. "Is your husband here?" Before I could speak, my husband tumbled in, dripping and blowing his nose.

We watched as he struggled to untangle his backpack from his dripping jacket. Finally, he dumped the clump of confused things, and we followed Dr. Laude into the examining room..

"There's a growth most likely from the stomach."

"Just tell my husband!" Her face reddened.

"I think you're hot," she morphed into my mother if my mother had cared about anything other than art.

"I don't want to know anything!" Then I lay on her table, ruining the white paper with my wet jacket, imagining normal people sitting motionless as they absorbed the fact that they have terminal GI cancer.

"The good news: the other organs are unaffected. There's an over fifty percent chance it is cancer but likely treatable," she said in a rush, like the news would get worse if she didn't get it all out quickly. The room flew around, and I begged to leave while she described the next procedure. Then I begged to stay, and then we left.

As we drove, my cell rang.

"Thursday morning and don't eat for twelve hours." My husband ticked off the horrors of Thursday morning: general anesthesia, a scope with a sonogram at the end, and a retractable needle. Dogwoods--my favorite tree--flew by and so did Victorian houses I still marveled at after thirty years in Providence.

By the time we arrived home, I didn't want to tell anyone that I was about to die, feel their pity, and admit the truth that they would win the race of living the longest. Defeated, I woke Thursday with my husband snoring at my side and so anxious I no longer felt my heart pound or my shortened breath.

"Great, great that we got you in!" I nodded, hoping this doctor couldn't hear my pounding heart. "So, so tough, but we wrestled the schedule to the ground!" She reminded me of our senior class president who got kicked out of Latin for cheating, and I wondered if she did well enough in her residency to stick scopes down people's throats, especially scopes with a needle and a sonogram at the end. Normally, I would have exuded enthusiasm as a technique for gleaning information, like where she went to medical school and had she performed this procedure nine billion times. But the anxiety rendered me mute. I did manage to ask if she'd only tell my husband the results. "No, no, no! You'll hear everything from me and no one else. No one else!"

Perhaps "anxiety disorder" was written on my chart. Why else would the anesthesiologist, a gaunt man with a kerchief tied around his head, tell me not to worry as he aimed a needle at my upper arm?

The next thing I knew, an annoyed nurse said I'd asked her the same question a million times.

"Oh," I said, my brain floating like a big soap balloon with me inside. For a while I stared at a blinking light until I realized my husband was missing. I tried to ask for him, but a voice told me that he was being consoled and couldn't muster the courage to tell me the news. I fell back on the pillow that defied any impression of my head.

One after the other, people in pastel colors passed the end of my bed. Each time, I asked for my husband, but no one heard.

"My husband is lost, I think." I wasn't sure why I came up with that explanation for his absence, but I guess I felt lost without him in this forest of wires, beds, machines, and people in ugly uniforms.

"She thinks her husband is lost." Someone squinted at me before hurrying away. *He's always in the wrong place*, I thought.

As I listed all his faults, he appeared.

"Where have you been?"

"Downstairs--no one came," he said, adjusting his side bag out of which his computer cord dangled. I smiled without smiling and tried again to sink into the rock-like pillow. He remembered that I'd appreciate a lie over the truth about my disastrous prognosis.

"Have you talked to the doctor?" the nurse asked as she handed us both juice boxes.

"No," my husband said, stabbing the mini straw into the small hole in the apple juice box.

"We haven't?" I wondered if anyone heard me as words continued to linger in my mouth.

"You don't like apple juice," I said. He tossed the box in the trash, and the doctor appeared.

"Never, never have I seen anything so unusual and nothing, nothing to worry about!" She'd pierced my stomach wall, pierced the blob, got some liquid, and now she was energized by the discovery of nothing.

"I mean, I have to send it to pathology, but that's weird. Weird!"I stared at the red embroidery on her pocket, *Dr. Lyder*.

Over the next week, nothing to worry about turned into an obsession with the pathology report, especially when Dr. Lyder didn't call the following week.

"Call her," my husband begged. As I turned on my phone, I screamed at the message: CONGRATULATIONS! YOU WON THE HAMILTON LOTTERY. I screamed again but this time in horror, at this being a warning that I'd been granted a last wish.

"Only one in ten thousand wins," I said.

During the four-hour drive to the Broadway theatre, I composed my obituary: "Although the prognosis looked positive, the pathology revealed a rare cancer caused by pressing blobs. In a miraculous turn of events, Smith won the HAMILTON lottery but collapsed at the curtain call. In lieu of flowers, please make a donation to The Pressing Foundation."

HAMILTON vanquished the real world. At intermission, I ran to the bathroom. In line, I stared at women with Pilates honed figures and others sagging, but all alive. Joy drained from my own fit body. What did it all matter: exercise, diet? Everything depended on the delayed pathology report. Like being stuck in a never-ending line, the pathology report was stalled, foreshadowing a lethal result.

Just before my turn arrived for the overused toilet, my phone buzzed. As I sat down, I tapped the green button.

"It's Dr. Lyder. Sorry! But this just popped up in my Inbox! All clear, all clear! Just a weird act of nature. The pathology shows nothing, nothing."

"Thank you, thank you! I'm relieved, I'm relieved."

"I'm sure, I'm sure."

I ran past the line of women, the line of men, the concessions. From our seats, my husband waved both arms like a traffic controller. I waved as the lights dimmed and a new chapter like a rainbow-hued bubble expanded around us, protecting us indefinitely, at least until the lights came up.

WHERE AM I?

"Hi, Louise!"

"Hi! See you later!"Louise yelled, squinting at a small hand waving to her from the backseat of a blue Volvo station wagon. Probably a kid in Ballet I, a class she'd teach that afternoon. Kids called to her all the time as she walked the Boulevard. Sometimes a parent would pull over to ask if she needed a ride. But this morning as she stalled, hoping Susan, a new friend, showed up for their morning walk, traffic along either side of the Boulevard was sparse. No one else yelled her name as she lingered. It almost seemed like a holiday.

She and Susan had walked the path in the middle of Blackstone Boulevard for about six months--ever since they'd met at a grants workshop. Then, about a week ago, Susan didn't show up. She also stopped answering Louise's texts.

Louise's phone fell into the dirt as she retied her shoe. She grabbed it, faked getting a call, and then called Susan. *If she answers I'll say it was a mistake.* Susan's message had an official tone like she'd had it professionally recorded. *Tacky,* Louise thought, telling herself she never wanted friends. She had an adequate boyfriend and lots of friends she snared and then released into something more like an audience.

As she pocketed her phone, a woman in a pink running suit adjusted her Fitbit.

"Good to stretch before a run," Louise said, planting her foot halfway up an oak tree.

"Sure is," the woman chuckled as a car like Susan's pulled up to the curb. Louise's heart raced. If Susan got out should she act like nothing had happened or beg for forgiveness for whatever she'd done?

She remembered the day near the end of the conference when Susan told her she liked her choreography.

"It's unique," she'd said as they sipped coffee during a bathroom break.

"Stems from a highly dysfunctional mind," Louise said as Susan stared without laughing or even smiling. "I just love to choreograph," Louise admitted, her heart quickening in the aftermath of this blatant truth. Susan's face registered nothing, and Louise grabbed her water, draining the glass like she'd just run a marathon.

"I can't figure it out, but your dances seem real--for lack of a better description," Susan said, aiming her crumpled coffee cup at a garbage bin. Louise nodded, wracking her brain for a funny rejoinder or a return compliment.

Try texting her, a voice whispered in her ear as Louise forced herself not to correct the woman's awkward stretching. Just last night, during their walk, her boyfriend told her to stop fixing his slightly splayed right foot.

"This is called 'a walk' and I'm not your student," he'd said. Louise's brain had buzzed with worry about a walk full of all small talk.

"Have a good run," Louise blurted as the woman yanked herself to standing and took off.

Memories of her walks with Susan flooded her mind as she made her way along the path. She pictured herself entertaining Susan with stories of her odd growing up. She remembered Susan chuckling at Louise's hyperbolic talk. Then Louise would ask Susan a question about her boyfriend or about working for Artists Behind Bars, nodding and saying *yes, wonderful, yes* without listening, her mind consumed with appearing interested as she formulated the next question.

And then, it dawned on Louise as she waved at a neighbor struggling with his puppy, that her orchestration of their banter may have felt wrong to Susan; the proportions were like a duet she once choreographed. One dancer did all the lifting and lugging while the other waited to be released.

Then Louise thought of the girls she'd marveled at growing up who traveled in pairs, disagreeing and agreeing effortlessly, like counterpoint in the Baroque music choreographers loved, music she found with its many counts and perfectly concluded phrases completely impenetrable. In graduate school, she'd been required to make a dance to one of Bach's concertos and by the time she finished, she felt like she'd been buried alive, something Chopin—her favorite composer--feared.

Maybe Susan was the exception to the rule that people love to be entertained when they're not being told that everything they've ever done is interesting and noteworthy. Louise's face heated, imagining everyone she'd ever encountered secretly thinking her a fraud for her constant interest in their lives and her words so often a repeat of their own. Louise shuddered, remembering a moment when she got caught agreeing with Susan one too many times.

"Are you my clone?" Susan asked, and Louise noted that now and then she'd force herself to disagree with Susan. But the mere thought of shaking her head or saying *no* to Susan or anyone other than her students, made her uneasy, so she'd decided to fill up their time together with more jokes and wild stories.

Louise left the path at an intersection, and then, in the middle of the empty street, she turned around hoping she'd see Susan back at the tree stump where they often retied their shoes. She imagined herself on her knees begging Susan for forgiveness. She squinted but could see nothing other than drifting leaves and a couple of squirrels tearing around a tree stump.

Without thinking, she headed down a hill toward a busy thoroughfare that separated her neighborhood--the East Side--from downtown Providence. At the bottom of the hill, a man wearing blue scrubs put a foot into the street, pulling it back as traffic roared by. He glanced at her, surprised, Louise thought, that anyone else would try crossing where there was no light. She wondered if he was about to commit suicide when she showed up, ruining his plan. For once, she didn't smile, just stared ahead as the two of them waited for a break in the traffic.

The man threw his cigarette and took off. Louise followed envisioning the two of them flattened and oozing blood. Her boyfriend might wonder if they'd been having an affair. She felt like grabbing his hand as they leapt onto the opposite curb. They walked at a clip toward a blinking *Walk* sign and at the corner, he turned into a bank, leaving Louise alone at the edge of Providence's downtown.

Up ahead, she could see a mess of one-way streets and No Parking signs. A woman wearing a hard hat slipped through some Jersey barriers and into the revolving door of a new building. Louise paused, hoping the woman might reappear. It seemed like everyone in downtown Providence was hiding, including the sun, which slid behind the only cloud.

Louise moved on, despite her brain advising her to turn around and go home. There was a church in the next block. She could chat with the secretary, feigning an interest in the stain glass windows. As she got closer she saw that the doors were chained and a sign hung from the doorknob with words smudged like mascara after a sweaty performance.

At the next light, Louise turned onto a narrow street, lined with parking meters, each with a blinking red violation light. Two pigeons showed up and she followed them as they jaywalked towards a fluorescent sign for Adult DVDs and lingerie. A cluster of birds landed near the two pigeons like they'd found their leaders. None of them noticed Louise--even when she walked straight at them. Out of nowhere, a man shuffled toward her with an outstretched hand. She shook her head and crossed back to the other side of the empty street.

She turned the corner at a Suboxone Clinic and found her reflection in a bank of mirrors. Signs advertising cheap rents flapped against some of the mirrors, blotting out her reflection. When a car sped out of a parking garage, Louise stopped. A neighbor who knew everything about Providence had told that she never goes downtown because parking was nonexistent.

"I *am* downtown," she whispered, laughing aloud and then again as she envisioned herself somewhere else, like Hartford or another city she'd never visited. She'd moved to Providence from New York because her then boyfriend began a Ph.D. program at Brown, but after ten years the downtown remained unfamiliar.

Louise whirled around. She decided to retrace her steps back to the East Side. She wished her footprints would appear. She tried running, remembering the day Susan took off and Louise followed, passing her.

"I'm just not a runner at heart," Susan called to her, bending forward, hands on her knees.

"No worries," Louise had said, unsure if she should be a runner at heart, or not.

Ahead, Louise made out the cupola on top of City Hall. Wouldn't it be weird, she thought, if Susan materialized? Susan, after getting a late fee, often paid her taxes at City Hall. Louise had told her that she, too, put off everything until the last minute as a voice in her brain reminded her that she paid her taxes ahead of time, before she even got the notice.

She ran for another block, skidding to a stop an inch from a wide, oily puddle. A dark rainbow framed Louise's reflection and she closed her eyes. Perhaps Susan hated her bulbous German features. If she'd worn makeup, Susan might've enjoyed her presence. Good-looking people go farther in life, she knew from some article in *The Times*.

Louise stepped over the puddle and squinted at the sign for Orange Street. Underneath was written in gold letters: Providence: The City of Hope. She sensed she'd come to the rim of downtown, like she was about to fall off into another neighborhood she hardly knew. But then, just as she thought she might crumple to the sidewalk, a man in a navy blue wool coat and shiny black shoes stepped out of a glass door.

"Do you know the best way back to the East Side--from here, that is?" Louise ran her fingers through her tangled hair.

"Not sure. Sorry," he said, checking his phone.

"Thank you," Louise said, deciding that from that moment on, she wanted to be known as someone who said *please and thank you* and never spoke to strangers. Then a police car going a million miles an hour with its siren on rounded the corner and the man looked up from his phone

"Out of control," he said looking at Louise with wide eyes.

"Totally!" She was about to say something else as he walked the other way. She thought about following him when she noticed, off in the distance, the Kentucky Fried Chicken she knew was on the East Side or at least at its edge. She ran towards the colonel's face, as his black eyes, bowtie, and the black letters expanded until the big fluorescent sign turned abstract, like paintings done by mostly men mid-century. Paintings she knew she was supposed to like by artists she couldn't, at that moment, recall although Lawrence of Arabia popped into her head because of his hallucinations in the desert. Some relief swept over her when Peter O'Toole's face, coated in sand, faded and she remembered a painter's name, *Robert Motherwell*. She smiled. Nothing she thought made her happier than storing away tidbits of information she could pull out of her hat while designing conversation.

Louise darted once again across the busy street, narrowly escaping being hit, this time, by a truck that changed lanes at the last second. The driver blasted the horn and Louise jumped onto the curb, losing sight of the KFC as she stumbled and, for a moment, lost her bearings.

"Where am I?" she whispered, wanting to scream. Instead she squeezed together her lips, fearing that the kids, kicking a ball in a parking lot, might run home to tell their parents about a wacked-out lady roaming the streets, talking to herself.

She remembered the time she'd told Susan about a crazy lady of her youth--didn't tell her that the lady was her mother. She'd recreated a scene with this lady who, out of the blue, threw her purse at a neighbor (her mother had thrown a chair, but that seemed too violent). In Louise's telling of the story, the neighbor dodged the purse and then hurried inside, reemerging a second later with a tray of Toll House cookies.

"Take one," she'd said to Louise. "Take another one for that poor woman." Susan loved the description of the woman throwing the purse. She asked if the cookie was good, since

Toll House sounded, to her, so much more delicious than regular chocolate chip.

Louise had tucked the story away, like all successful stories, but now she panicked because she couldn't remember if the Toll House part had happened, like she was mixing everything up. From now on, Louise told herself as she spun around to find the KFC, she'd be simple and polite and also she'd live in the present--literally the moment at hand.

"Run," she yelled. She obeyed, pounding her feet into the sidewalk, ignoring everything her high school track coach had told her about rolling through the foot. Streets she crossed, like Lancaster and Woodbine were familiar mainly because her old boyfriend had lived on Lancaster. *You spent a lot of time there,* she reminded herself as sweat dripped down the sides of her body and her eyes watered.

Everything was blurry, but she'd know her street when she got there. Her teeth chattered and she worried, they'd never stop. It would be tough, impossible really, to teach dance with chattering teeth. Finally she saw the ugly blue house on the corner of Oak and her street, Summit Avenue. She recognized her neighbor's car coming toward her.

"Hello," she yelled running to the car. Her neighbor put on the blinker and turned before Louise got to her. A dog barked at Louise from behind a fence and she screamed. Then she saw her house and she slowed down like it might disappear if she ran at it, the way birds fly away if you move quickly.

The house was dark. She peered in the window, checking that the furniture was hers. Inside, she stood in the foyer, waiting for her heart to slow down and her teeth to stop chattering. Then her stomach growled.

She'd make lunch with anything she could find--omelets, perhaps. But she found the egg carton at the back of the refrigerator, behind a bag of potatoes and Louise couldn't imagine rearranging things in order to slide out the eggs. She'd let her hands and feet thaw before tackling lunch.

She closed the fridge and pressed her back to the door. Her heart refused to slow down, even with slow breaths. Louise tried to smile at her ridiculous position as a refrigerator magnet. Would someone find her in this absurd position? If her boyfriend discovered her glued in place, she'd break up with him. He might refer to it in the future and by the afternoon, she hoped to start over, forget everything about the day so far.

She caught sight of the CD player flashing. She must have left on the Donna Summer CD. She decided to move just far enough to turn it off. *One, two, three: MOVE,* her voice yelled, echoing throughout her head. She thought of her brain like a cave and all her thoughts as bats careening off the cave's sides and ceiling. A cave was a horrible image, she decided, and tried to erase any thoughts of emptiness. Finally, she obeyed the voice and inched away from the refrigerator but she pushed the FM button instead of the CD button.

Louise recognized one of the Chopin Preludes playing on the radio. A piece of music she'd danced to costumed in men's black work boots, a white tutu, and bare legs. She'd loved this dance, mainly because the work boots disguised her stiff feet-- strong but not curvy in the least. She was still obsessed with the requirements of classical ballet even though she'd developed her own jerky stiff style that people seemed to love. Watching the video of this solo recently, she'd admired her spoking bug-like limbs that seemed to match the neurotic fluidity of this Chopin Prelude. One of her creative movement students had called it *Bug Dance*.

The moves came back to Louise. She wasn't surprised. First of all, she'd choreographed the dance in this very same kitchen, and all her movements were essentially the same--rigid in the limbs and fluid in the backbone. But the Chopin had brought out something different. She remembered jumps and turns--exuberant traditional moves she hadn't chopped out. And now she threw in new steps, threw in every step or movement that came to her. Then she edited her movements, cutting out everything except the simple tossing of her hands upward, as she began to undulate her spine. *I bet Susan would like this*, she thought.

BRING THINGS OUT IN PEOPLE

By the time the doctor—the only dermatologist in Rhode Island taking new patients--barged into the dingy exam room, I was determined to find another dermo, even if it meant going to Boston. During my first appointment I'd found his wandering left eye disconcerting, but worse was his suggestion that my flirtatious past would be my downfall.

"Look," he'd said as he washed his hands, "you've probably done stupid things like sunbathing--anything to get the boys flocking to those blue eyes. Well, now you pay." I noticed his neck muscles flexing under the crisp collar of his white shirt.

A month or two later my husband found another mole on my back. I prayed this mole, like the last one, was just a nerve ending that had surfaced.

"So you've got kids?" He slapped my folder on the shelf, ignoring both kids huddled on my lap. As my chart slid to the floor, I wondered if I brought them for protection.

"Yes, I do."

"Melanoma? A lethal killer," he said, a note of satisfaction creeping into his voice. Then he got about an inch from my face, one eye staring into my eye and the other moving toward my ear. "You're an absolutely perrrrfect candidate for skin cancer." His lips parted and he'd stepped back, taking me in.

"Debbie, please come give me a hand, I've had an accident." He clicked off the intercom and swung around, his face turned to the small window at my side so that his good eye faced me. He frowned, ignoring my son's smile.

"So the problem today is a mole on your back?" He stepped closer, kicking at the file on the floor.

"You said if a mole changes or feels different I should have it checked." He sought my eyes before walking behind me. "I mean I can't see it but," I waited for him to finish the sentence.

"I'll lift your sweater and check for cancer."

"Thank you," I murmured, wondering if cancer would be the punishment for returning to this guy. *Slime ball* I thought, worrying that I was exaggerating. Maybe he was just weird and nothing more.

"Stop," I whispered as my son pinched my skin. The doctor echoed me in a low voice--like a whisper between the two of us. Then he lifted my cable knit sweater, inching it upward. I shivered under the light pressure of his knuckles on my back. I was about to plead for an answer, when he sucked in a lot of air and screamed like he'd never seen a case of melanoma so advanced.

"Mommy!" My daughter jerked backward, banging her head into my cheekbone, and my son mimicked the doctor, screaming as he yanked my hair.

"What is it?" I whispered, trying to erase a picture of the kids next to my grave.

"You don't have a bra on," the doctor said, dropping my sweater.

"I know, but is the cancer too advanced for treatment?" The hum from the overhead fluorescent lights filled the room.

"You're still safe; it's another nerve ending that's surfaced." My son, who was riding my knee, waved strands of my hair, and the receptionist flung open the door.

"Debbie, you should respond to my calls quicker. Her records have been on the floor for a while."

We drove home, the kids in their car seats and me squeezing the steering wheel. A squirrel ran in front of the car, a sign I thought that I'm more squirrel than human since they, too, don't think before acting or not acting. Like, why didn't I tell the doctor to go to hell?

After swerving around a slowpoke station wagon, I jerked to a stop in the driveway. I froze as the doctor popped up in my brain and I imagined him saying, as I buttoned my blouse, that being around me drove him crazy.

"Sorry," I said to my sleepy kids. As I pulled back the food-encrusted straps of their restraining seats, I caught my daughter's eye. What if she thought I wanted the doctor to talk about my underwear? For a moment I imagined her as an adult shaking her head at me.

"I can't believe you didn't tell that creep to go to hell."

"But I never *did* anything," I begged for forgiveness as she looked askance.

"This just pisses me off," I said, shaking a head of half-dead lettuce over the sink like it was a wet rag and not the fragile organic lettuce grown in greenhouses. "Hydroponics," I whispered, trying to focus on how few of the green leaves were usable but instead looking backward at a replay of the dermatology appointment so that I didn't see the little vase of dandelions about to tip off the windowsill above the sink.

"Shit!" The thin glass shattered into a layer of sparkling shards across the bottom of the stainless steel sink. The week-old dandelions landed in a clump over the drain, already full of soggy beige cereal and dead lettuce.

"Piss and shit," my daughter said from the den.

"Those are grown-up words," I yelled, without sounding convincing.

"Who wants chicken tenders?" I could see both kids staring at the TV, the baby from his wind-up swing and my daughter curled up in a corner of the couch. I was relieved to be ignored and turned on Frank Sinatra singing, "Come fly with me, let's fly, let's fly away." I smiled at what once passed for naughtiness as I pictured my dad, after a shower, walking around the house naked, garnering the attention he craved for his own beauty. He joked about joining a nudist colony where everyone lived free.

I grabbed a bag of chicken tenders out of the freezer and danced on the balls of my feet around the kitchen, flopping onto a stool after I hit my shin on the open dishwasher door.

"God damn it," I winced, rubbing the bare bone.

"God damn it," my daughter said from the den as a voice on the TV announced that secondary cigarette smoke kills children.

"That's enough!" I yelled as the phone rang. Before I answered, I waved at my daughter, who waved back, reminding me of my vow to protect her from grown-ups everywhere, especially those who smoked and talked about bras and I guess, walked around naked.

"You're not going to believe what happened to me," I said into our black cordless phone as I poured myself a glass of white wine. The woman on the other end had clung to me at a neighborhood party a few years back. I often thought of getting rid of her--her know-it-all personality drove me nuts.

"I think you bring things like this out in people," she said after I whispered the story into the phone. My face burned as I told her I had to get food in the oven.

Bring things out in people, I said to myself as I slid the cookie sheet covered in a layer of jumbled chicken tenders into the oven. I had once worried this accusation could be the case, when as a teenager in short shorts and a cute crop top, I found the optometrist's bald head resting on my bare thigh. In my blind and dilated state, I hadn't moved, not knowing what to do with a head pressing into my flesh. Even after racing home on my bike, taking a shower, and changing into a maxi skirt and a blouse, I couldn't get rid of the feeling of that head. Seemed like it was there forever.

I opened the newspaper, hoping a good story would rid me of my friend's scolding and the guilt welling inside. More Frank might help, too, I thought as I got the CD going again. I leaned against the sink, positioning myself under one of our overhead recessed lights, shining down on a story about a bombing in the Middle East.

But instead of concentrating on a photo of a woman in a long skirt and scarf, cradling a limp teen-aged boy and the headline, A DAY OF RETALIATION, I dropped the paper and thought of his eyes--actually one eye--staring into mine. I remembered my husband saying that I was the most beautiful woman he'd ever seen. He'd had too much to drink at the time and I figured that he *wanted* me to be the most beautiful woman. I sunk into the sink, my heart beating in my temples. I came back to life when I smelled the tenders.

"Dinner," I shouted, pulling the cookie sheet of half-frozen, half-steaming chicken pieces out of the oven.

"He's asleep." My daughter pointed back to the baby slumped in the swing as she tiptoed into the kitchen.

I smiled and stroked her hair

"You're such a help!" She nodded, stretching her mouth into a gargantuan smile. I admired her blonde curls and her light, delicate walk. People say we look alike, which somehow made it worse that she'd heard the dermatologist talking about my bra during the appointment.

"Mothers take kids to doctor's appointments all the time," I said aloud. She nodded.

"Milk and ketchup?" She raised her eyebrows. I got the milk carton out of the fridge, edging it between two half-empty cups of juice.

"Where's the ketchup?" I muttered, before spying the half-empty ketchup bottle behind the pitcher of lemonade. How many times had my husband asked me to put things like the ketchup bottle on the shelves tucked into the refrigerator door? I promised myself I'd organize the refrigerator and keep it neat, actually establish some normal habits that might make up for my bringing things out in people, which my flip-flopping stomach equated with disloyalty, a trait my husband never displayed even when our neighbor pretended to care about his tomato plants, going as far as gathering her long flowing skirt so she could better inspect the rows of his run of the mill beefsteak variety.

My daughter, bored with eating, slipped to the floor to play Snow White. She waited for my kiss. I knelt under the table where she lay amongst the crumbs and the streaks of dried tomato sauce on the wall.

As soon as I kissed her, she opened her jaw, and a chicken tender fell out. Then we galloped around a stool, the two of us on the same imaginary horse.

When the backdoor banged shut, I yelled to my husband that I loved him. When he came into the kitchen, I pressed myself against his chest and he stroked my hair. Our daughter stood on a stool and made kissing noises. He let go of me and swung her high, her feet grazing the overhead light. *I love him*, I said inside my head, fingering my wedding ring. The dermatologist's face appeared hanging in the air next to my husband.

"We're quitting the dermo," I blurted.

"Why?" my husband asked, setting our daughter on the stool.

"I don't trust him," I said, wondering, as my husband lifted his eyebrows, if he, too, thought I brought things out in people.

CHRISTMAS EVE DAY

I was in the kitchen on Christmas Eve day, Johnny Mathis blasting on the boombox, hands deep in a bowl of sugar cookie dough. My five-year-old daughter nibbled raw cookie dough and licked up the tiny colored balls you sprinkle on the cookie before the icing dries. Instead of making the perfect Christmas, I was yelling at her to get her tongue off the counter. She smiled, her lips and teeth decorated, but without the icing.

Anyway, just as I smacked the sugar cookie dough, the house shuddered, and we froze.

"Did you feel that?" Karen nodded as she sucked on a wooden spoon. Then we ran through the house, me clutching the rolling pin and Karen the tub of cookie decorations.

I struggled to grip the doorknob with my greasy hands. Karen tried, but by then the knob was covered in a greasy film. I wrapped my bathrobe around the knob and that did the trick--the door swung open.

"Who's there?" Karen whispered as I clung to the threshold with my toes, and she braced herself against my leg like we were about to fall forward.

I squinted hard at a blanket of steam rising from the snowless sidewalk.

"Brave new world," I said, waiting for the fog to lift or my eyes to adjust to six o'clock light at noon. Like a horror movie soundtrack, the porch floor creaked, and I realized the porch floor was no longer flat but slanted toward the street. Could the house be tipping over? Karen and I crept forward, gripping the floorboards with our bare toes.

"There's a car sticking out of the house!" Karen yelled. I screamed as the porch fell an inch or two more, biting into the car's metal top. Karen leaned over the railing, her stringy hair nearly grazing the car's bumper.

"Make love not war," she said.

"You can read that?" I grabbed onto the back of her nightgown.

"Listen," Karen said, jumping into my arms. Someone under the porch grunted and said something about strawberries.

Karen slid to her feet and together we watched a woman with long wavy hair crawl on her stomach, one foot caught behind the old Buick's heavy door. Her purple dress bunched around her wide thighs, letting us see the straps of her white garter belt pinching the tops of her stockings. I wondered if I should cover Karen's eyes.

The woman struggled to stand in her black pumps. Once upright, she stared into our house through the open door, like she belonged here and was trying to remember why she'd left the front door open. Or maybe she was too embarrassed to look at Karen and me in our pajamas. After easing herself on to one of the old marble steps, she lit a cigarette she pulled from a leather bag.

My eyes followed the curling smoke as it floated toward the street. I noticed my neighbor's peach tree on its side--roots like gnarled fingers. Next door, a geyser of water spurted straight up. And then, as my eyes circled further, I saw a shiny silver jeep lying on its side, smoke seeping from under the hood.

I knew I should do something, call 911, for God's sake, but I became catatonic as thoughts swirled in my head about my house's possible involvement in a street-wide disaster. I had just read an article in the *Providence Journal* that said INTENT IS NOT NECESSARY. You don't have to want to kill someone, it explained. You don't even have to really kill someone. You just have to get the ball rolling or be in the wrong place.

"Got a little rheumatoid," the woman said, exhaling a stream of smoke.

"Rheumatoid," Karen said, nodding.

"Going to get some strawberries for the church social--that's all." Out of nowhere, a guy appeared, blood smeared across his forehead.

"Do you need help?" I asked, praying he'd shake his head. I had witnesses, after all, who'd attest to my solicitation.

"I'm fine," he said, walking backward and pointing at the jeep still on its side. "But my car, my car," he trailed off as he disappeared around the corner.

Karen saw the small hand first, reaching up and then clinging to the old marble steps, still stable and erect in the middle of the collapsing and splintering porch. Then a leg swung over, and a boy in khaki trousers and a blue blazer rolled on to the steps. Five, maybe six, I decided, as he stood in front of the woman with his head bowed. She nudged her feet to one side, making him a place without looking at him like the two were strangers, arriving separately as the Trumps often did for a speech or something important.

"I can't do this," she said, flexing her foot. "Can't because of the rheumatoid." Karen joined in, flexing her bare foot. "He should have listened instead of always being so excitable." Again, with eyes straight ahead, she talked to no one. The boy dropped his chin. I nodded, worrying that I should be hugging the boy or at the least whispering in his ear that it was okay to be excitable.

"Why he pressed his hand all the way to the floor when I'd told him go easy. His hand has got do the work for my foot. So why he pushed his hand all the way down, I don't know." Karen took my hand as if to show the woman what hands were for or at least what they weren't for. The boy's back stuttered and he covered his face.

"I told him, crouch low and go easy with the fingers." She nodded, pin-wheeling her fingers and smiling like she was an old pro at hand acceleration. Meanwhile, the boy sobbed.

"Don't cry." Karen slid next to the boy as a police car came around the corner, followed by a fire truck. The police officer and the firemen jumped out, leaving their doors open, and I wondered if a city-wide law stipulated that doors be left open during emergencies.

"We don't want an explosion!" A fireman yelled as the policeman shouted for us to get the heck away from the house.

"My god," I imagined the entire neighborhood in flames--hundreds of people dead.

"Whose car is this?" The policeman pointed at the bumper sticker. "Whoever the driver is comes with me." The woman ground her cigarette into the old white marble step and then she and the boy followed the policeman. Karen wrenched her hand from mine and ran after them.

"Can't he stay?" she begged, grabbing the boy's hand. The policeman ignored her and pointed to the inside of the car.

"Get in," the woman said to the boy, shooing him inside. Karen waved at the car and then covered her ears when the policeman put the siren on before racing away. Across the street, neighbors formed a line and many took pictures with their phones. Out of nowhere, a tow truck backed up on to the front lawn.

"What are you doing?" I yelled at the tow truck operator as he hooked the submerged car to the truck.

"You've got an explosion on your hands!"

In our pajamas, we huddled together, Karen rubbing off bits of dough that clung to my hand. A boy across the street yelled her name and she waved. Then, in a violent lurch, the crunched and ruined car emerged, and the porch collapsed amidst a mess of tangled spindles. Karen cried as she pointed at a bag of frozen strawberries on the other side of the shattered windshield.

"The strawberries--they forgot the strawberries," she wailed.

A MAGNET FOR THE WEIRD AND DESPERATE

I never open the front door to anyone, not even to someone I know. When I hear knocking, the first thing I do drop to the floor and crawl like a baby. Sometimes I log roll. The reason for this is simple: our front doors have windows from the waist up. Believe me, in my next house there aren't going to be any windows, at least not in the doors. Anyway, once I am eye to eye with the weather stripping, I scrunch onto my knees, hold my breath, and lift the flap over the mail slot just enough to peek at the person's face. If I don't know the person—wouldn't know them if they were sitting in my soup--I lower the flap and wait for whoever it is to leave. But even if I know the person, I refuse to open the door unless someone else is home. You never know if this friend or acquaintance has had an out-of-the-blue personality change. If that's happened--and believe me, it can--at least someone like my husband can verify that it's not me who's turned into someone else.

You may scoff at the idea of a friend's or an acquaintance's metamorphosis, but as a magnet for the weird and desperate, I've experienced just that. Sure, the weird and desperate usually are the unfamiliar. Take, for instance, the two guys who put a curse on our house when I wouldn't pay them to repair one of our banged-up cars. Just a little FYI: They relented on the curse once I gave them the requested paper products along with a carton of milk. I think the carton of milk clinched the deal. One of the guys guzzled it down, straight from the spout.

But don't think the weird and desperate are always the unfamiliar. One morning I woke to wild pounding on the front door. In a panic, I ran down the stairs, pulling on a bathrobe. Through the window, I saw a tall, unshaven neighbor also in his bathrobe. Up to this point, I'd only seen him in a suit, even at the pool club.

"Hi, Bill." I hoped that was still his name.

"Can I borrow one hundred dollars right now?" He talked to me through the window like I was a bank teller. "Ellen is on fire on 95. That is, the car's on fire. I need the money to have her towed home. The car, I mean, with her in it. Oh, and…small bills would be better."

Or how about the time my sixty-five-year-old neighbor, a children's librarian who always wore Birkenstocks and flowing moo moos, appeared on my porch in a leather mini skirt and cowboy boots nuzzling and kissing her teenage daughter's boyfriend? They wanted to know if they could take a drink out of our hose, which I thought was really polite. If I'm thirsty and I see a hose, I'll just take a drink.

So why then, on a balmy afternoon in late November, did I open the front door to a total stranger? How, in a matter of seconds, did I go from a totally sane, normal human being to a rash, unthinking whack job?

Here's how it went:

I was in the kitchen making dinner. My twelve-year-old daughter was, as usual, practicing the piano in the front parlor. My son was at basketball practice. My husband was in the middle of a three-hour seminar, coaxing students to stay awake and discuss *Giants In The Earth*. (I don't know what's wrong with these students. I love books about mentally ill people, and books with mentally ill people stuck in prairies are even better.)

Anyway, without any warning, a person taking too literally the sign DOORBELL DOESN'T WORK. PLEASE KNOCK LOUDLY, began banging on the front door right through, or should I say over, my favorite Chopin Prelude (Agitato) that my daughter Priscilla played with particular feeling. I rushed to the door with a head of dripping lettuce in my hands. Something about the Chopin mixed with the loud knocking, mixed with visions of the bleak South Dakota prairie, persuaded me to confront this loud-knocking person head-on. No crawling, no log rolling.

Through the window, I stared at a very tall man in a too-small jacket waving my checkbook back and forth. I knew it was my checkbook because of the dried egg yolk on one corner--a stubborn splotch I'd tried very hard to wash off. I'd even tried scratching it off with a nail file, slicing my index finger. Fixated on my checkbook, I began to unlock the door when this man coughed--without covering his mouth.

I jumped back and covered my mouth. Although I'm afraid of very few things, I am afraid of tuberculosis. But something about this man's gaze against the background of steam rising from the street on that tropical winter almost evening, reminded me of the terrible finality of everything in *Casa Blanca*, and I unlocked the door and offered the man my wet hand. He held on tight. Priscilla stopped playing the Chopin, and, in the silence, the three of us waited for something to happen, like the end of the world. Finally, he spoke in a rich baritone.

"I found myself sitting on a bench behind Hope High School quite a distance from here, when I reached under the bench and my hand hit upon this checkbook, which I believe is yours. I've walked far and wide to hand-deliver it." He paused. "I could have, after all, simply slipped it through the mail slot."

I gasped, picturing the checkbook sliding through the slot, hitting the floor and our family forced to evacuate rather than risk potential exposure to anthrax or other types of lethal contamination. He widened his eyes, nodding. "You may think my effort extraordinary, but to me, it is called honor. Plain and simple."

I heard the ominous tinkling of a few low notes—very reminiscent of the young girl being sacrificed in *The Rite of Spring*.

"You walked all the way here? How can I repay you? I haven't been able to find my checkbook since… yesterday!" He smiled, revealing straight yellow teeth with sharp incisors. Also yellow were the whites of his eyes, and I did my best to block out the symptoms of hepatitis that echoed through my brain. "Someone must've slipped a hand into my purse, taken my checkbook, and then stowed it under that bench with a plan to return for a few checks, but only now and then." We both raised our eyebrows, me about an eighth note after him. "No one would suspect someone of cashing another person's checks at random intervals." He peered over my shoulder as he stepped toward me, one foot on the threshold.

"My thoughts exactly, Madame. You've read my mind." He cleared his throat, gazed upward, and as if he knew we'd memorized Emma Lazarus' poem engraved on the Statue of Liberty in a last-ditch effort to persuade our son to participate in Poetry Week, he lifted his palms.

"Give me your tired, your poor, your huddled masses yearning to be free." Priscilla from the parlor piped up:

"The wretched refuse of your teeming shore, send these the homeless tempest-tost to me." I finished, beckoning him inside:

"I lift my lamp beside the golden door!" He bowed, his tiny jacket cinched around his armpits.

"Oh, won't you come in? It would be an honor to have you enter our house and rest your weary feet. You must be exhausted and hungry!"

"Both." Then we cocked our heads, listening to Priscilla run through a progression of chords, all in a minor key.

"What are you doing?" She mouthed as we passed her on the way to the kitchen. He smiled, slipping off his child's jacket. I caught it and raced after him. I found him sitting erect at the island as if he'd lived in our house in a former life. I worried it had been neater then.

"Cookies?" I asked.

"For starters, certainly." I arranged a plate of chocolate chip cookies I'd made with ground flax seeds, a supposed cure for my husband's high cholesterol, and asked if he'd like some coffee.

"If it's freshly brewed." He looked askance, eyeing the cookies before selecting one. "Not quite enough sugar," he said, shaking his head and raising his eyebrows like the guy on the British Baking Show describing the failed efforts of one of the losers.

I began to heat the water, when out of the corner of my eye, I saw his long thin fingers inch along the counter toward my checkbook. Instinctively, I grabbed it, noticing that not only were the whites of his eyes yellow, but one pupil was blue and the other gray, and they both seemed to be spinning. Then he stood up and began to intone in a deeper voice.

"Give us this day our daily bread and forgive us our trespasses as we forgive those who trespass against us!" He lifted a cookie above his head, breaking it in half. We gazed upward as crumbs rained down and the teakettle began to hiss, spitting water in all directions.

A few scorching drops hit my face and I screamed, imagining this man baptizing me in scalding water. Death by scalding was not something I'd ever worried about, but I was terrified of brainwashing, and now I found myself in danger of being hypnotized by asymmetrical eyes and biblical quotes. He chuckled, at what I wasn't sure, but in my mind, a scene unfolded in which he laughed, clutching his sides as I ran along a desolate dirt road, lost in a country where hepatitis and tuberculosis are rampant. In the final scene, we're missionaries, and half of my face is covered in a violent red burn mark.

"And lead us not into temptation," he shouted as he slipped a cookie into his shirt pocket.

I was considering, begging this man for forgiveness for any number of sins when Priscilla tiptoed in, and the phone rang. I grabbed the receiver as if this was my last connection to the world as I'd known it. Sort of like the ending of *Casa Blanca* when she's about to board the plane for heaven knows where.

"Hello?"

"It's Corinne from the church." I gulped hard for no reason except that my dance studio is located in a church, and although I had encountered the secretary once or twice between classes, I'd never gotten the woman's name straight. I couldn't be sure this Corinne was the secretary or someone perhaps in cahoots with the eye-spinning man or perhaps someone else altogether--a representative from a worldwide kidnapping agency hell-bent on placing disfigured missionaries in remote locations.

"Just want to let you know something sort of disturbing. Someone has been in the church stealing things and well, doing something else. This person forged some of Father Buber's checks and also took the communion wine. Whoever it was played all your Tchaikovsky CDs. I know this because they were scattered everywhere, and one, "The Waltz" from *Sleeping Beauty,* was playing on your boom box, and something else was on your boom box that I don't feel comfortable talking about. It could remind someone of glue, only with a bleach-like smell. Rhymes with emasculation--that is, the production of it. You're going to want to check all your things and don't forget to bring some paper towel and disinfectant."

I whirled around as the man clinked his coffee cup against the saucer.

"I hope you have cream for the coffee. And by the way, could I request some Tchaikovsky from the young pianist?"

ABOUT THE AUTHOR

MARY PAULA HUNTER came to writing as a performance artist fusing text with dance. Her debut novel, SOMEONE ELSE (2019) has a five-star rating on Amazon and was selected by Kirkus Indie Editors to be featured in the Kirkus Reviews (June 2020). Her writing has been called "brilliant" by The Village Voice and The Manhattan Spirit. CAN I HAVE A HUG FIRST? was published by GULF COAST online (2018). HEAVEN a flash fiction piece was published in FLASH FICTION MAGAZINE (2016). GROCERY STORE, submitted to Glimmer Train placed in the top 3% and was awarded Honorable Mention. Hunter gained her perspective on middle graders and high schoolers through raising two children and running a dance studio for many years. She lives in Providence, RI with her husband Brown University historian, Richard Meckel.

ABOUT THE PRESS

Unsolicited Press is based out of Portland, Oregon and focuses on the works of the unsung and underrepresented. As a womxn-owned, all-volunteer small publisher that doesn't worry about profits as much as championing exceptional literature, we have the privilege of partnering with authors skirting the fringes of the lit world. We've worked with emerging and award-winning authors such as Shann Ray, Amy Shimshon-Santo, Brook Bhagat, Kris Amos, and John W. Bateman.

Learn more at unsolicitedpress.com. Find us on twitter and instagram.

www.ingramcontent.com/pod-product-compliance
Lightning Source LLC
Chambersburg PA
CBHW030006010826
48973CB00009B/2683